Old Palmetto Drive

by

S.E. REED

Wild Ink Publishing
wild-ink-publishing.com

Edited by Brittany McMunn and Nicole DeVincentis
Design and Layout by Abigail Wild

ISBN (paperback): 978-1-958531-62-4
ISBN (epub) 978-1-958531-57-0

*For my husband and children—
my loves, my inspiration.*

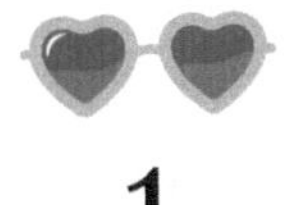

1

NEW YORK PRINCESS

MOM IS SUCH A fake. She cried and screamed at Dad when he said he was leaving her six months ago for Heather. But I knew Mom's dirty little secret. She already had divorce papers locked in the top drawer of her desk. Ready to whip them out and slap Dad across the face when the moment was right. She kept the key in the bottom of her jewelry box under a picture of her sister, my Aunt Kris... A place Dad never thought to look. A place I looked when I dug through her jewelry and dressed up to go out one night.

Maybe Dad knew it was coming. He is a Wall Street guy, after all. You know, smooth and polished, always gets what he wants. I'm sure being married to the most powerful divorce attorney in New York City made him think about divorce once or twice. Well, Mom *was* the most powerful divorce attorney in New York City.

Yesterday was her last day at the office. She really is, like seriously is, making us move to Everglades City, population four-hundred fifty-six.

Swamps and alligators.

Rednecks and Confederate flags.

Banjos and howdy Ma'ams.

No shopping malls for a hundred miles.

Even the ocean shoreline sucks, covered in something called mangroves. Which means no beaches.

I hate her.

"I still can't believe Mom is making me move to some trashy swamp town in Florida," I complain to my best friend, Ava, as I push open the double doors of my penthouse bedroom and drop my vintage, black-stitched, Fendi bag by one of the boxes. I ceremoniously kick off my Gucci slides, letting them fly across the room before I pull my long blonde hair up into a top knot. I hate that sweaty feeling behind my ears.

"Rian, how far is the swamp from Miami again?" Ava asks as she sprawls out on my king-size bed. Her dark hair cascades across the white, goose-feather pillows.

My lips curl into a scowl. "I told you, Everglades City is super far from Miami! It's like driving from here to Philly or DC. I don't know. Someplace stupid and really far away." I walk over to the mirror and reapply my Dior lip oil.

"Ewe, that *is* so far. I still cannot believe this is happening to you," Ava sympathizes. I glance over my shoulder and watch the corners of her mouth turn down like she finally realizes the gravity of my situation. I'll be over a hundred miles from any major metropolitan city. For a born and raised New Yorker, it's pure torture.

"Mom says there is a silver lining. She says moving to the country will be therapeutic for us," my voice drips with sarcasm. "She said New York is not the center of the world, and I need to get over it." I plunk down on the edge of my bed.

Ava and I look at one another and burst out laughing.

"I think Tori's been hitting the Chardonay a little hard," Ava teases and lifts her hand to her mouth with a pretend wine glass and throws her head back like she's sucking it all down in one gulp.

"A little?" I smirk. It feels good to laugh with Ava, especially at Mom's expense. Everything has been so grim and serious lately, which makes this move even harder. "Not the center of the world," I mumble again and frown.

Mom's wrong.

New York isn't just the center of the world. It's the center of the universe. It's the *City that Never Sleeps. The Big Apple. The City of Dreams.* New York is my entire life. My friends. My school. *My Dad.*

A tightness sits in my chest when I think about how much I'm going to miss New York. I go over to the mirror above my desk and pull out my Dior Mascara. I slick on another coat of the rich, midnight blue, forcing myself not to shed anymore tears because tears and Dior don't mix.

I watch Ava in the mirror's reflection as she snuggles deeper into the mountain of pillows on my bed... I bite my lip. I think maybe she will look up at me with a tear glistening on her own cheek, scared to lose me as much as I'm scared to lose her. Instead, she just gets on her phone.

I look back at myself, normally a view I like to admire, but right now I look like shit. You can tell I've been crying every night since Mom sprung the Florida news on me a week ago. I put my hands to my face and hope no one noticed how tragic I looked at school.

"Gross! I look like I've been on a bender for a week. I'm breaking out and I didn't even have time to get my roots redone. I'm sure there won't be a salon anywhere close to swamp town either," I complain. "Oh my god. Will I have to do my own hair?" I imagine holding a bottle of cheap hair color to my head and gag.

"And your own nails too. Better stock up on polish," Ava adds without looking at me. I look down at my pink, gel-manicured nails.

"FUCK!" I slam the mascara tube down in frustration.

Ava's smiling at something, casually twirling her dark hair with her free hand. Then she sits up and holds her phone out to me. "At least you aren't Gina. Her new Gucci slides are so fake! How embarrassing. Should I tell her?"

I look at Ava, then at the image of our friend Gina with her fake Gucci's. "Yes, you should tell her. What if it was you?"

"First of all, I can spot a fake a mile away. And second, you're no fun when you're in a bad mood. The *old Rian* would have laughed at that picture," Ava whines.

"The old Rian?" I ask her.

"Yeah. New York Princess Rian. Now your Florida Rian," she says all matter of fact.

Me, Ava, Gina, and Maggie are the New York Princess-es, aka NYP's. Every weekend we dress up and go dancing or shopping or out to eat. We hit up the spa and go to the movies and have sleepovers. We do almost everything together. Partially because we can't stand to be apart, and partially because we all want what the other girl has. Sure, we each have our own interests, like Ava with her violin and Maggie and horse riding. Maybe Gina can't spot a fake Gucci, but she is a superstar gymnast. We've been my best friends for as long as I can remember. The thought of leaving them is worse than the thought of coloring my own hair.

Mom told her assistant Darcy I should be grateful because in Florida I might "find myself" and not be so spoiled. What the hell does Mom know anyway? What a stupid thing for her to say. Maybe I like myself and my life just the way it is. Honestly, this entire move feels so unnecessary. One stupid little murder-suicide and suddenly everything has to change.

Okay, I admit, maybe I am spoiled. But how can Mom expect me to be happy or excited to leave the only life I've ever known?

"Seriously, Rian. Just tell your Mom you're not comfortable living in a house where your relatives died because there might be ghosts. Tell her you want to move in with your Dad." Ava puts her phone down for a second and looks at me encouragingly.

"God, Ava, don't be such an idiot. Mom knows that kind of stuff doesn't scare me. I mean, I barely knew my Aunt and Uncle. And if I could stay with my Dad, don't you think I would? He's not even in New York. He's in Berlin on some huge project for work and won't be back until the end of summer, plus Heather is with him." I roll my eyes. Sometimes, it's like Ava isn't listening when I talk.

"Well, you could just call your Dad and cry and beg to go to Berlin with him for the summer instead of Ghostville. The guys in Germany are super hot." She turns back to her phone.

"Going to Europe defeats the purpose, Ava. I want to stay in New York with you and the NYP's! And you know my Mom will never let me live with Dad as long as Heather is around." I rip the ponytail holder from my hair and run my fingers through my mane.

"Maybe I can come to Miami and hang with you for Spring Break next year. I'm sure my parents will fly me down," she says trying to change the mood. "Look at this gold bikini. It would look incredible on me." She holds up her phone again.

I don't look.

I'm literally moving a thousand miles away and all she cares about is her chance at Spring Break in a #Gold-Bikini.

Damn her.

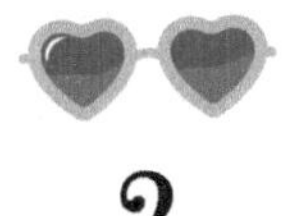

2

DEATH IN THE SWAMPS

"YOU GIRLS WANT TO order dinner for your last sleepover?" Mom opens the double doors to my room without knocking. She knows I can't stand it when she barges in on me. I glare at her as hard as I can without making my eyes bleed.

"Thanks, Ms. Callusa I'm starving. Can you order pizza from Patsy's and do you have anything sparkling?" Ava asks in her annoyingly sweet voice, the one she uses to get her way. "You know I can't drink plain water."

"Of course, Ava, and how about some anti-pasta and fresh cannoli's with the pizza? I think we still have some Pelligrino in the fridge. I'll go check," Mom replies in the same annoyingly sweet voice.

God, they both make me sick.

Then Mom smiles at me with her perfect, every man on 5th Avenue wants to take her home for the night, smile and blinks her big eyes like Katie Perry. "Anything special for you Rian?"

I shake my head no, and she walks out, closing the doors.

My face burns. The audacity of her to act so fake. I want to scream, but instead throw the closest thing I can find on the floor, my old American Girl doll, Lanie. She slams against the door with a hard, plastic thump and Ava jumps.

"Rian, you need to relax."

"Shut up, Ava." The door to my room opens back up. I expect to see Mom telling me to grow up, but it's just Darcy, Mom's utterly devoted personal assistant. "What do you want?" I snap.

She folds her arms and looks around my room. "Whoa Rian, haven't you even started packing? We are leaving in less than twelve hours." Her voice is cheerful and her eyes are bright. I guess she's looking forward to the trip. At least someone is.

"Why should I pack?" I flop onto my bed.

She picks up Lanie from the floor. "Because your mom is going through a lot right now. The least you can do is be a big girl and pack your own suitcases," Darcy replies.

I give her an icy stare as she oh-so-gently puts Lanie into my Louis Vuitton side bag and zips it up.

"Yeah, well I'm going through a lot right now too."

I put my headphones on so I don't have to get any further lecture. Darcy shrugs and walks out. I look around at the mess. I guess she does have a point, maybe I should start packing my stuff for *Murdertown.*

I told Ava it doesn't bother me that we're moving to a house where my aunt and uncle died. But, I guess it is kind of creepy. I mean, what if there are blood stains on the floor? Or bullet holes in the walls? If it wasn't for my two hillbilly cousins, Sam and Travis, we'd never be moving there in the first place. Mom inherited *them* and *their house*. It's the same house Mom grew up in that's been in her family for generations. Look, I know what people must think. Any sane person would fly down to sign the custody papers and bring my cousins back to live here with us in New York. End of story.

But no, not Mom.

She decided it would be best to keep things simple for Sam and Travis; the same high school and their friends and sports. Sam is going to be a Junior, and Travis is going to be a Senior next year, just like me. She said the trauma of what happened to their parents and finishing high school and applying for colleges will be hard enough on them without dealing with big city life. But me, who cares, right? Make me leave my city, my friends, and my life! She decided right after she got the call about Aunt Kris...without even asking me how I felt.

We were sitting on the white leather sectional together in the living room, watching an old classic movie, a thing we used to do sometimes, when her phone buzzed. "I better take this," she said and jumped up and walked into the other room, sliding the big pocket doors closed behind her.

I knew something was wrong the moment she came back and sat next to me. "Rian, I have horrible news." Her eyes were damp, and she smelled salty, but not in a good way, like after going to the beach. More like in the way you smell when you're scared. "Aunt Kris and Uncle Chuck are dead."

"Mom, oh my god!" I leaned over to hug her. She wasn't shaking or sobbing. She was eerily calm. As if she'd expected something like this to happen. "Was it a car accident? A plane crash?" I asked, trying to make sense of it.

She took me by the shoulders and looked at me with those haunting, black eyes. "No, much worse. Rian, pack your bags. We are moving to Florida."

"What? No way! I'm not leaving New York." The words had flown out of my mouth with such rage. Every bit of empathy and sadness I'd had for my mom losing her only sister vanished when she said we were moving.

"No argument. Chuck finally did it. The bastard killed her. We leave in one week."

That was it. She didn't care that next year was my Senior year. She completely disregarded all of my hopes and dreams for my perfect New York life. The next few days had been a blur preparing for our departure. It was like I had stopped existing. Like our life in New York had been the thing that died, not my hillbilly relatives in a trashy murder-suicide. People she never seemed to care about.

Until now.

I start packing my suitcases, carefully placing my designer clothes in color-coded order. I feel sick with each handful that goes in. I can't even look at my rows of shoes placed neatly on top of their boxes. Does Mom even care if they get scuffed when I rebox them? And my bags and purses! Oh god! Sweat beads around my hairline. I might have a panic attack... I'm sucking air in faster than I can exhale it. Seeing my custom-built walk-in closet in disarray is making my head spin.

I sit on my bed, trying to calm down. Ava is happily texting someone and smiling, completely ignoring me. I slump forward and put my face into the white duvet, debating if I should just start screaming.

My stupid bed.

I don't even get to take it with me. Mom said Aunt Kris's house is filled with extra rooms and tons of furniture, so we aren't taking any of ours. Instead of screaming, I get up and walk out. The apartment used to be filled with art, statues, and modern furniture. The perfect Manhattan penthouse. Now the furniture is draped with white sheets, like ghosts.

I open the door to Dad's old office. He was in such a rush to divorce mom he didn't even take any of his shit. It's the one room, besides mine, that Mom hasn't finished packing. I look out the window at the city skyline before slumping into his desk chair. I am going to miss this view so much.

"Rian, why are you in here? Are you okay?" Darcy bounces in wearing workout gear and her hair in a high ponytail. She carries a box labeled ASSHOLE and starts pulling things off the shelf, dumping them in without any regard. Probably just to haul to the trash. Mom thinks she's so funny.

"No, I'm not okay. What do you think?"

"Honestly Rian? I think you're being unreasonable. If you could have a little sympathy for what your family is going through, it would make all of this a lot easier, on everyone."

I spin my Dad's office chair away from her and look out the window again. I know she's waiting for me to say something cruel. But sometimes silence is just as effective. She gets the point and doesn't say another word to me. Once she's gone I pull out a pencil and piece of paper from the desk. I start drawing.

The one thing Mom and Dad always agreed upon is how talented I am as an artist, but that's where their agreement ended. Dad said art was a hobby. Mom said my talent should be cultivated. Mom wanted to put me in art school. Dad said that was too much pressure. They'd argue in circles, both trying to get the upper hand. Meanwhile, I was out partying with Ava or shopping with Gina. I stopped showing anyone my artwork a long time ago. What's the point? It's not like I'd ever be taken seriously in the art world, look at me, oozing privilege—the exact opposite of a starving artist.

I keep sketching anyway, trying to calm down and let myself get lost in the graphite on the paper. Shading the buildings, etching the windows. The NYC skyline. It's my city. My heart sinks. I guess it's not my city anymore. I crumple it up and throw it across Dad's pathetic home office.

I hate being so angry.

How convenient for Aunt Kris to die at the exact same time when mom was desperate to start a new life after her divorce. I feel gross for thinking thoughts like that.

But I can't help it. I have to get out of here. The walls feel like they are closing in around me.

I need room to breathe and fresh air.

Maybe that's how Mom feels... Oh.

3

Shattered Glass

I OPEN THE DOOR to leave Dad's office and the smell of hot mushroom and cheese pizza is wafting through the hall, lightening my mood substantially.

"AVA!" I scream. She comes rushing out of my room.

"MMmmm! Is that the pizza?" Ava runs past me and out into the kitchen.

"God, she's lucky," I complain as I follow her. She can eat whatever she wants and still has a thigh gap between her legs. I barely think about food and start cupcaking over my Tom Ford jeans. What does it matter anymore? There won't be anyone to impress in the swamp. Just a bunch of hicks. For some reason that makes me feel better. I mean, the standards in a place like Everglade City have to be pretty low. I'll probably be the hottest girl in school and obviously I'll have the nicest clothes.

Actually, I'm not hating that idea. All the guys will want me and all the girls will want to be me. Or maybe the other way around. Either way, the odds are good for me.

Being the most desired girl in a new town? Yeah, maybe there will be some good things in Florida.

"Don't eat it all without me." I laugh as I walk into the all white marble kitchen and see Mom, Darcy, and Ava stuffing their faces. Mom's shoulders relax when I enter the room with a smile on my face. She puts down her slice and opens a bottle of wine.

"Do you girls want a teensy little sip?" she asks and winks at Ava who pretends to be shocked.

"Tori! But, we aren't old enough," Ava gasps. Of course me and Ava frequently pour ourselves glasses of whatever my Mom has lying around the house. Last weekend we drank an entire bottle of Dom Perignon with orange juice for breakfast when mom was at hot yoga. Our little secret.

"I want more than a sip. This is our last night in New York. I want the whole bottle." I walk over and take two glasses out of a box that's not sealed up. Why did she pack the crystal stems from her and Dad's twentieth wedding anniversary? The ones etched with their wedding date and last name. I might just have to accidentally drop–

"Ooops!" I let the glass slip from my fingers to shatter on the floor in a thousand crystal glass shards.

"RIAN!" Mom and Ava and Darcy shriek in unison.

I pluck another glass from the box and let it fall to the floor. "Ooops again." I start laughing. They all look so confused. I shrug. "What the hell do we need these for? To remind you of your divorce?" I point a finger at Mom. "Don't they use mason jars and drink moonshine in the swamp?" I grab the bottle of red wine off the island and take a swig right out of the bottle, then turn on some music.

Darcy's eyes are about to fall out of her head and Mom's mouth is open like a fish. I'm pretty sure they think I'm crazy. Maybe tonight, my last night in New York City, my last night in the only home I've ever known, is making me crazy. I start singing along to the lyrics–don't ask me how I know the song, but somehow I do.

I croon the country words. Darcy grabs a broom and sweeps to the beat of the music. Ava is still wide eyed from my display of temporary insanity. Sometimes it's like she doesn't even know me at all.

But Mom does.

She grabs my hand and sings along to the song, badly– "There's a hole in the bottle of wine..."

Pretty soon we are dancing and laughing. We eat Patsy's pizza and drink the last of the wine and talk long into the night about all the good times we've had in the city, like our constant trips to Central Park. Mom cries a few times and I cry with her. I know I'll regret it tomorrow when I remember I'm supposed to be mad at her, but for now, it's the right thing to do. Darcy falls asleep on the guest bed without any blankets and Ava escapes back to my room at some point.

Mom and I hug for the first time in a week while standing in the kitchen on the remaining slivered shards of broken glass.

4

JUST TEXT ME BITCH

"UGHHHH! MY HEAD IS pounding," Ava complains the next morning as she sits up in my bed.

Her hair is matted on one side where she was drooling and pushed into the side of me. I have this entire king size bed and Ava always wants to be right up on me when she sleeps over. She says it's because her Au Pair held her every night in bed until she was ten. But, I think it's because she knows I've always had a bit of a crush on her and she likes to torment me.

She's my best friend. I don't want to ruin it by demanding some stupid love affair that would never work out. She's not into girls, and even if she was, I couldn't deal with dating her. She's such a drama queen most of the time, okay all of the time– a real New York Princess. She's the reason we named our group the NYP's in the first place. Like, seriously, she bosses everyone around like they are peasants. And my parents think I'm the spoiled one.

I really hate how much I'm going to miss Ava. How much I'll miss this, waking up with her clinging to me. Even when I pretend to be annoyed. Even when I think she's a bitch. She's my bitch. My best friend. Now, what, she'll be with Gina and Maggie everyday? They will probably forget all about me and move on with their own stupid, privileged lives and I'll wish I was here with them every second.

"Rian... I need water and ibuprofen." She holds out her hand like I'm supposed to get up and go get it for her. See what I mean?

"Quit complaining. You're usually such a lush," I tease her.

"Shut up," she moans.

I pat her head softly. Then like a dutiful friend, I get up and find her some Ibuprofen and a bottle of Perrier. I hand it to her and she flashes me a half smile before curling back up into the covers. I walk to the bathroom and look at myself in the mirror. I expect to see a monster looking back at me. I only got a few hours of sleep, but surprisingly, I don't look that bad. I wink at my reflection.

"You got this," I say to myself before I shower.

Mom and Darcy are in my room packing up the last of my things when I exit the bathroom. I don't argue or tell them to get out, partially because Ava is still curled up in my bed nursing a headache and partially because I need all the help I can get. I put my make-up and sketch pads in my suitcase and sit on my bed until Mom and Darcy are done.

"Come on, Ava." I nudge her leg. "Your mom will be here any minute, and I think we are done here."

"I don't wanna," she moans.

"And you think I do?"

She drags herself from my bed and sulks all the way to the kitchen. I stand in the doorway not sure if I should say some kind of prayer or what. Instead I take a farewell selfie of me and my room.

Five minutes later, while Darcy and Mom lug the last of the suitcases and boxes into the hallway, Ava's mom shows up to take her home. We stand awkwardly amongst the chaos, saying goodbye ten thousand times.

"Look, it's gonna be fine," I say and hug Ava again.

"Let me get another picture," her mom says.

"God, Mom, stop it!" Ava sobs. "You're making this so much worse."

"Hold it, right there." She angles her phone.

I can't take another second of this. "Just text me bitch."

"Bitch." She laughs and sniffles.

We hug one final time and I squeeze harder than I ever have before, then flash her the peace sign. She glances over her shoulder as she walks onto the elevator. I memorize the way she looks, fragile and sincere, so completely unlike her.

When I'm alone later I'm going to sketch her with that look on her face, the smeared mascara from sleeping and crying, the glassy, red eyes.

My heart aches.

After our farewell, I walk back inside. I could use a few minutes alone, but Mom stands with her sunglasses on her head. "Okay Rian, now that you've said goodbye to Ava, are you ready to go?" She holds my bag out to me. "Darcy is going to follow us in the Range Rover. Do you have anything else you need to load up before we hit the road?" Mom claps her hands, emphasizing each word.

"Nope." I cross my arms over my chest. I'm back to being angry and bitter. Whatever moment we had last night has completely vanished.

She stares at me with a smile, as if I didn't just mouth off.

I glare at her.

"Great! Let's get this show on the road, kiddo. I'm sure Sam and Travis are anxious for us to arrive and the housekeeper, Mrs. Day, can't wait for me to get there and take over parenting duties." Mom grabs her keys.

We walk out of the penthouse for the final time.

Neither of us look back.

Mom's excited about what lies ahead.

I'm too broken to turn around.

5

FRIED OKRA

IT TAKES TWO DAYS to reach South Florida. I spend most of the drive looking at my phone and ignoring the change that is taking place in Mom. She has always been the picture perfect New York mom with a powerful job. But a few days of driving back to where she came from is changing her and she's becoming something I don't recognize. Her tight ponytail has been let loose and the windows of her black Mercedes-Benz 700 series are down with the music blaring. She's been listening to Garth Brooks on repeat for the last hundred miles.

"God, Mom, this song is so annoying! Change it already."

Instead she turns and asks loudly over the chorus, "Do you wanna have lunch at Cracker Barrel?" There's a twang in her voice I've only heard once before when we went on a family vacation with Aunt Kris, Uncle Chuck, Travis, and Sam. I was eight and it was the first and only time I ever met my cousins. When we got home to New York, Dad said he would never take a family vacation with Mom's family again. Mom sobbed hard that night, you know with real big sloppy tears and gasps.

"Eww, Mom! Cracker Barrel? That sounds like a place you have to have a mullet to eat at. Yuck. I am not eating there. Isn't there a sushi place? Or bagels or something?"

I bury my nose back into my phone at the pictures my friends are posting. Today is the last day of school at Trinity. Mom took me out of school early. I cried and begged to stay for the last two days, but did she listen? NO. Now look, Ava is posting perfect last day of school pics with Gina and Maggie and I'm not there wedged in the middle where I belong. I'm stuck in this car driving to hell.

"I have been dying for some fried okra ever since we left the city. Now, let me tell you, nothing is as good as what they fry up at Cullier Manor House, but this will do in a pinch," Mom says and whips the car across three lanes and off the interstate.

"Jesus Mom, are you trying to kill us!" I scream.

I look in the rearview mirror. Darcy is still behind us after pulling an equally terrifying lane change. "What in god's name is Cullier Manor House?"

"That's the name of the place we are moving to. I know I've told you about Cullier Manor House. It's on Old Palmetto Drive. You know, the farmhouse from the picture in the guest bedroom," she reminds me.

Oh yes, that creepy antique black and white picture of a run-down, two-story southern farmhouse.

"Why didn't they live in their own house?" I ask, sort of interested, I guess.

"When our parents died they left the place to us. I had no interest in it and signed my shares over to your Aunt. She worked her butt off restoring it. She used to send me pictures of all the renovations and work." Mom looks proud as she pulls into the parking lot. "Kris always had an eye for that sort of thing, interior design and antiques. She could have had a career in it, but she was too busy making sure Uncle Chuck didn't fuck up the family business and taking care of the boys."

"MOM!"

"What? Chuck was a pain in the ass piece of shit. Look what he did."

It's the first time Mom has mentioned *what Uncle Chuck did*.

Murder.

—⁓⁓—

"Sheesh! Tori, you drive like a maniac!" Darcy says to Mom after we park and walk up to the front of the restaurant. The place is like a roadside freakshow with rocking chairs and checkerboards lining the giant porch. Everything is foreign to me.

"Sorry Darc, I'm starved. The okra and sweet tea are calling my name," Mom says and puts her arm around Darcy. "Come on, let's eat."

Okay, so I have to admit, it is sort of cute and kitschy once we get inside. It smells warm and cozy. I put my headphones on and pretend like I'm not listening to Mom and Darcy talk while we eat. I poke the grits and nibble on a biscuit while they are deep in some kind of work discussion.

"I've given your offer a lot of thought," Darcy leans across the table and tells Mom. "You can't run the company and raise three kids alone after everything that's happened. You need me." She picks a french fry and holds it up.

"Darcy, you are my angel," Mom says and picks up one of her own fries. They tap them together, like they are clinking wine glasses for a big toast.

Company? What company? That thing she said about Aunt Kris and the family business? I pretend to eat the fried okra, okay maybe I really eat it. What can I say, it's good. Then I pull out my sketch pad and work on a sketch of the waitress. She's wandering around asking to refill everyone's sweet tea. Her teeth are too big for her mouth and she keeps flashing them at every table. The entire time I'm sketching her I think, how can you be happy to be a waitress? What a pathetic job.

Mom and Darcy are still busy yapping about this business thing and I'm only half paying attention. Because guess what? I don't care.

"Okay, so like we discussed. I'll increase your salary by twenty-percent and you can live with us, the rental market in Everglades City is pretty limited." Mom pulls out her ipad. "I'll draft a contract right now and email it to you. Just e-sign and send it back to me so I can have the corporate attorneys work out the rest. I can't tell you what this means to me."

"I would do anything for you, Tori! You are the only reason I finished law school last year. I'll take the Florida

Bar as soon as I'm able. I won't let you down," Darcy replies.

Oh, just lawyer talk. They are probably starting up their own law firm in Florida. BORING! I yawn.

"Looks like someone could use a nap while we drive the rest of the way. I'm sure your cousins will be excited to show you around when we arrive, so you probably should rest, Rian," Mom says.

"I'm almost seventeen, Mom. I don't need a nap." But of course the moment we get back into the car, I curl up in my seat and fall asleep.

6

That's the House?

"Rian... Rian Callusa. Wake up. We're here." Mom gently shakes my shoulder.

"Hmmm. What?" I lift my head and look around. Where am I?

She's driving slowly down an old road lined with huge palm trees. We approach a massive, black rod iron gate that's shut. There's a brick guard shack on one side and security cameras pointing everywhere. This is not what I was expecting. Where's the old house from the black and white picture? She didn't say anything about a security checkpoint. Mom's car comes to a stop and she rolls her window down.

"Well ain't you a sight for sore eyes, Miss Tori!" An old man with white hair and bushy eyebrows half-way up his forehead, says through the window. He exits the little booth to come closer to the car. His suit is too big on his small frame and I frown. "The boys are so excited to see you. They be wound tighter than a girdle on a baptist—they keep callin' down askin' if y'all are on your way to the Big House." His thick Southern accent is so heavy I can barely understand him.

"Well heavens me Robert! Kris didn't tell me you still worked here. I'm so happy to see you," Mom replies.

Heavens me? Really mom.

"Yep, forty years last September. Now, lemme see that pretty girl sittin next to you. Must be Miss Rian. You the spittin image of your Mama when she was a young lady." Mom leans back so Robert can get a good look at me. I hate being put on display. Like, I'm not a toy poodle or something.

"Hi," I say quickly, then turn my back on him to look out my window.

He laughs deep.

Mom doesn't skip a beat and just continues. "Robert, can you call up to the Big House and tell them we've arrived? I promise to come down and have a nice visit with you once we get settled. I wanna hear all about how you've been. Tell Mabel I want her to come 'round for some sweet tea on the porch."

Come 'round?

Sweet tea on the porch?

SERIOUSLY! Who is this woman, and what has she done with my savvy, New York Mom? I spin back and look at her. She flashes that stupid pretty smile at me and shrugs.

"Righty, Miss Tori, that sounds good. Now, don't let me hold you up any longer," Robert says and goes back into the booth. He pushes some buttons to make the gate open and waves at us as mom drives forward.

"Really, Mom?"

She sighs.

"Rian. This was my life. The people here, I grew up with them." She takes off her sunglasses. I guess she wants to take in the view in full color.

"So what? Just because you're from here doesn't mean you can start acting all weird," I tell her and shake my head.

"Rian, you don't get it do you? This place is my legacy, it's going to be *your* legacy. I guess I didn't understand or respect it until I ran away from home to go to law school in New York. Even then, I didn't see the value, the love, the warmth until it was too late. I'm not about to fuck this up now. So yes, I'm going to use every bit of kindness my New York heart has left to make up to these people. My people. And someday, your people too. After everything that's happened, I just hope it isn't too late. Now, when you meet your cousins, I want you to remember something... You might be grieving your life in New York, but these boys, they are grieving dead parents."

"God Mom, you act like I'm some heartless bitch." I shake my head and huff.

"If the Jimmy Choo fits."

"UGH!" I snarl at her.

She ignores me and drives the rest of the way up Old Palmetto Drive. My legacy? What the hell was that all about? I close my eyes for a moment, afraid to look as the car makes it around the last bend. I hear her breathing speed up. Then she says, "I'm sorry I wasn't here sooner... "

I know Mom's not talking to me.

She's talking to her dead sister.

I reluctantly open my eyes and look around, to see what exactly has Mom all anxious. Towering before us is Cullier Manor House. It's like right off the cover of some Southern magazine. The place is massive with a huge porch. The hedges are trimmed, the crushed gravel is pristine, there's a three tiered fountain and flower gardens. There are at least twenty other buildings and small houses dotted along the expansive manicured property. This is some kind of wealthy compound.

"Welcome to your new home Rian," Mom says and turns off the car.

"What the–" I pause. "Mom. This is a mansion. This is not at all like that creepy picture from the guest room. I thought this was going to be some dumpy farm in the swamps, what the hell is this place?" I am seriously in shock.

Mom laughs. "That picture was from 1890. A lot has changed here since then."

"Yeah, no shit," I mumble.

Darcy parks behind us. I hear her door slam. Mom and I are just sitting awkwardly, not getting out, so I try to enjoy the last few minutes of A/C. Then Mom puts her hand on my knee and leans toward me.

"Rian, look at me. I need you to be on your best behavior. That New York attitude of yours will not work around here. Use 'please' and 'thank you' and 'yes ma'am' and 'yes sir' with everyone you meet."

"Oh Jesus mom, get a grip," I snap.

"RIAN!"

I get out and slam the car door. Who does she think I am? Obviously I know how to say please and thank you. I'm not a barbarian. I have more class than Mom ever had at my age. I lean against the car, but it's burning hot.

"Yep, this is hell."

I pull away from the scorching metal and put my hand up to shade my eyes from the late afternoon sun blazing down. I hear Mom's car door open and shut. I turn around to tell her I don't accept her apology for accusing me of having no manners when I see she isn't coming around to me. She's got her arm around Darcy and they point at the house, walking and talking and laughing. People rush to them and Mom is the Queen Bee. Just how she likes it.

Who are all these people anyway?

There's a man in dirty coveralls. A woman wearing gardening gloves. Two men holding shovels. A small woman with an apron standing next to a plump woman with gray hair. Gardeners, housekeepers, cooks?

I don't understand any of it. Why are there so many people here? What is this? Like a hotel? Is that the family business? Seriously, what exactly did Aunt Kris and Uncle Chuck do anyway? I thought they were country bumpkins.

Sweat spots form on my Balenciaga shirt and my pink, shredded slouch-shorts threaten to strangle me from the humidity. I fan myself, but the air is damp and something buzzes.

"Something just bit me!" I scream and slap my arms and at my face.

But no one is around to hear me scream. They are all fawning over Mom and Darcy who have made their way onto the porch. "Goddamnit Mom, you better have bug spray in one of the bags." I huff and open the trunk of her car. I'm waist-deep searching through the luggage when I hear the crunch of gravel as someone approaches me from behind.

My heart speeds up.

Eww, why am I nervous?

7

Circus Tent

"Hey, Rian," it's Sam or Travis, I can't tell from the voice.

"Hello," I say slowly and pull my body from the trunk.

The entire drive here I envisioned my cousins to be toothless hillbillies wearing trucker hats and flannel. Sure, I could have asked Mom if she had a picture of them. But, I didn't want her to think I might be interested in moving here.

This house it's not what I expected. So, my cousins probably aren't either. My knees tremble. I turn around and the boy in front of me is wearing khaki shorts, a baby blue Lacoste polo shirt, and leather strap flip flops. He's about as tan as a country boy is supposed to be and has sandy blonde hair.

It's Sam.

"Hey cous! Glad you made it," he says. "Travis is out in the garage. Got tired of bein dressed up and waitin for y'all. He's workin on the Camaro, the one dad used to drive. You wanna come see? You got taller since last time I saw you," Sam talks nervously and blushes.

"Oh," I grumble. "Yeah, taller."

Sam smiles. It's the same smile Mom has, the perfect one, and he probably uses to get out of trouble. He looks like trouble with that dimple in his cheek. For some reason the fact he's so perfect makes my blood boil. I smile back, even though I want to scream at him that I'm pissed off and I don't want to be at Cullier Manor House. I want to go home to New York.

"So, you wanna go see Travis?" he asks again. He shifts from one foot to the other.

"Um... sure. Can I go inside first and put my stuff down?" I ask, then turn back to Mom's trunk and grab my Louis bag. Oh shit! I forgot to take out the Lanie doll. I'll have to put her in the trash or hide her under my bed before anyone sees her. Sweat beads roll down my forehead. I'd reach up to wipe them off, but I'm holding my bag awkwardly with two hands. I feel like an orphan clinging to my only possessions, ready to go see my room at the orphanage.

Why is it so humid here?

I think I might throw up I'm so hot and sweaty.

Mom's laughter from a distance trickles our way and Sam says with a frown, "Her laugh is the same as Mama's used to be." His eyes go dark. He's the orphan. Not me.

"I need air," I manage to squeak. I feel faint.

"Gosh cous! Where are my manners? Let me take that bag for you and show you and Aunt Victoria inside and get you cooled off." Sam reaches out and takes my bag.

"Sounds like Mom and Darcy are still busy talking to everyone. You can just take me," I tell him. I'm desperate to get inside and out of the heat. The sound of bugs is so loud it feels like my ear drums might explode.

"Well, what do you think of the place?" He asks as we walk.

"It's...different. There are a lot more people here than I expected," I admit to him.

"Yeah, it sure is somethin, ain't it?" Sam says proudly.

"Yeah," I mumble. I mean, it is impressive, but I'm not prepared to give him the satisfaction of saying so.

"Mama always said Aunt Victoria would come back one day. Said this place was in her blood. You can run from the South, but it will always call you home," Sam says as he slowly opens the huge front doors.

For a moment, Sam is the Ringmaster.

He's oddly charming and looks at me like I'm the grand lioness he's about to unleash for the cheering crowd. But I don't care if this is a three ring circus, with clowns and popcorn and trapeze swingers behind the door.

"Whoa, what the fuck?"

The words escape my lips before I can stop them. I'm standing in a giant, circular foyer with a staircase coming down from one side. There's a marble topped table in the center filled with fresh cut roses and expensive art and statues everywhere I look. Someone is even playing the piano in another room, the music drifting in softly. If I didn't know better, I'd think I was standing in a hotel lobby in Manhattan.

"Come on, Rian, up here. Your room is next to me and Travis." Sam is already half way up the dark, rich-ma-hogany staircase. Oil paintings of fair Southern belles line the walls. The Persian runner lining the steps is handmade. The place smells like Scotch from crystal decanters and worn leather. Like the time I snuck into one of Dad's "secret" club meetings at the Metropolitan. That's where he and all the other Wall Street turds would hang out, eager to hear detailed accounts of who they screwed and how much they spent on their Maserati.

"Who are all these people?" I ask, stopping to look at one of the portraits of a pretty brunette with a scowl on her face.

"Our relatives. That's Gram Tweety when she was our age."

She looks like Scarlett O'Hara from *Gone with the Wind*. I only know that because Mom makes me watch it sometimes when Dad is out of town. Okay, maybe I ask her if we can watch it. So sue me, I like old movies.

"Mmhmm." I make a noise to acknowledge I heard Sam.

"Gram Tweety was a huge fan of Viven Leigh." Sam explains and continues walking to the top of the stairs.

Everything is just so– peculiar. Crystal chandeliers, fine art, antique furniture all polished and perfect. This place is like a slice of pecan pie. Mom used to say that when I was little and it drove Dad insane. He was born in Connecticut. In his mind, people from the South were backward. Whenever she said anything he thought was too Southern, he'd give her an evil eye. It was kind of tragic when I was a kid, but then I got used to it. My skin crawls, cause like, that is pretty shit of Dad when you think about it.

"It's like pecan pie," I whisper, just to feel the words roll around in my mouth.

"We have pecans. We can pick them this fall if you like that sort of thing. Mrs. Paula, the cook, she makes the best pie," Sam says as he opens one of the doors at the end of the long, upstairs hallway.

"Uh, okay. Sure," I say. I don't know what that means. Pick pecans. Like off the ground? From a tree? Do we have to climb it?

"Well, this is your room, Rian. Me and Travis wasn't too sure what you'd like, so we left it pretty empty so you can put your city girl touch on it." Sam smiles awkwardly.

He goes over and sets my bag down on the floor by the huge bed. Am I supposed to thank him or tip him? Now, it's my turn to smile awkwardly. Sam looks around the room and puts his hands in his pockets. Should I ask him to have a seat? To help me unpack? To get me a glass of water? Mom said use my manners.

"Thanks for showing me to my room, Sam." Then, before I can stop myself, I blurt out, "I'm sorry your Dad killed your Mom. Uh, I mean, I'm sorry about your parents." Palm to face.

Sam doesn't say anything.

"Sam! There you are. Let me get a good look at you." It's Mom. She lets out a sigh when Sam turns around to face her. "You are so grown up." Her voice is shaky and she wraps her arms around him.

"Aunt Victoria." He sobs into her shoulder.

"It'll be okay. I'm here now. Come with me, Sam, and let's let Rian settle in. How about we go catch up on the back porch." Mom guides a crying Sam out of my room.

That pain in my chest, the tight feeling I had before leaving New York, returns. Like an ache in my heart for the loss that is suddenly everywhere. Sam's parents are dead. Why on earth did I bring it up? What is wrong with me? I grab at my chest trying to make the pain stop.

But all I do is hurt harder.

"GOD!" I yell and slam my new bedroom door shut and run over to the window, seeking anything to take away the feeling. I look down through the glass and notice Darcy talking with someone in the yard, pointing at the fountains and flowers. There are people unloading everything from our vehicles. I don't know how long I stand there, in a daze, but it feels like forever until my phone vibrates in my bag– pulling me back to reality.

It's Ava.

More pictures from back home. She's such a bitch. Look at them! Her and Gina and Maggie eating ice cream and taking pictures at the Bethesda Fountain. They don't even miss me. I throw my phone down on the bed. I guess I could send a picture of the fountain out in my new yard. I go back to the window to look at it again. Not nearly as impressive as the massive stone water feature in Central Park.

That's when I see a flash of the late afternoon sun reflecting off something far out in the distance. I squint to see what it is. An old metal building. I bet that's where Travis is working on cars. I decide I'm going to go out there and tell him he better come inside and say hello. If Mom said I have to use my manners then so does Travis. The least he could do is greet us when we arrived. But, before I go marching out there with a bad attitude, I take the band out of my pocket to pull my hair up. The house isn't completely immune to the sweltering swamp heat and my neck is sweating and tingly from the salt oozing from my city skin.

I sigh.

Do I really want to go outside in the heat and find Travis right now? Not really. But, I'll go crazy if I stay in this empty room by myself. I look around, it's not really that empty. I guess the huge, white, four-poster bed is kind of perfect. My cheeks flush when I realize it's the same bedding I had back home. I wonder if someone ordered it for me? God, they must think I'm so spoiled. But, can I help it if I only like certain sheets and a very specific white duvet? What? My skin itches when I sleep on cheap fabric.

There's a white vase with Magnolia flowers on the nightstand next to the bed. And on the farthest wall sits a desk with a beveled, gold mirror hanging above it. I go over and sit down and look at myself. How many other people have looked at their own reflections while sitting at this desk.

I stand and head for one of the closets half expecting a ghost to jump out, but instead it's a huge, custom walk-in with a floral, rose patterned paper lining the shelves. Like the Gucci limited edition design from a few years ago. Interesting. I kind of love it. I'll have to sketch it later when I have more time.

And what's this? Another closet?

Oh my god! It's a bathroom. A claw foot tub gleams with gold feet and designer white towels with my name monogrammed on them. There's another vase of fresh cut flowers. Even the toilet paper is folded into a point. Why did Dad always say Mom's family were a bunch of white trash? Because if I didn't know any better, I'd say I was standing in a five-star hotel bathroom.

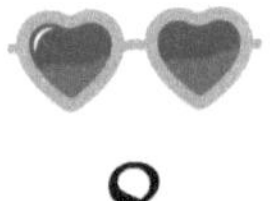

8

FISHING LURES

I'M STILL ADMIRING THE bathroom when I hear someone calling for me. "Miss Rian, are you in there? Pardon me if you're using the toilet."

"Hello," I reply and walk out of the bathroom.

There is an old woman with purple-tinged, gray hair standing in the middle of my room. She's wearing bright pink lipstick and an apron. I try not to laugh, but seriously. She's something else for sure. If Ava was here she'd double over at the sight.

"There you are. We've been waiting all day for you to arrive," she says.

"Um... yeah, we stopped for a long lunch." I shrug.

"Of course you did! Long journey from the big city." She puts her hands on her hips and bounces from foot to foot.

I nod and look around, suddenly nervous because I, uh, don't know who this woman is. My heart starts to beat a little faster, again, and for a split second I wonder if she's a ghost. She looks like someone who could be a ghost. I narrow my eyes on the edges of her. Don't apparitions have fuzzy edges like they are blending into the air?

"You look just like your Mama, don't you? I've been here for nearly fifty years, you know. Worked for your Gram. I watched your Mama and Auntie Kris toddlin 'round these halls. This used to be her room, your mama's."

When she talks I see lipstick on her teeth. I don't think ghosts can have lipstick on their teeth. I try to hide my smirk and my shoulders relax.

"I took the liberty of filling the bathroom drawers with your favorite soaps and shampoos and lotions. Your Mama's lady friend, Miss Darcy, sent a list of what to buy you. I got the sheets you like too. I wasn't sure how much you'd bring, leaving New York in such a hurry and all."

"Thank you Mrs..." I pause.

"I'm Mrs. Day, the housekeeper here at Cullier Manor House." She bends in a subtle curtsey when she finally introduces herself. "Anything you need, you just let me know. I have one of those fancy Apple computers and the boys set me up to order things out of that Google box," Mrs. Day says proudly.

Google box. Old people are so dumb. But, I guess she's trying. She did get me my favorite sheets. I can't wait to see what she filled the bathroom drawers with. Of course Darcy sent a list ahead of our arrival, such a suck up.

"So, this was my Mom's room?" I ask, fairly certain this woman is not a ghost and she seems eager to talk. I look around again.

"It sure was! Now, if I recall, she had it painted lavender and had all kinds of posters on the walls." Her eyes gently graze over the walls as if she's back in time, remembering it as it once was. "There was old carpet in here too. Course, Kris pulled up all the carpets and redid the floors. She done a real good job renovating this place. We have plenty of old photo albums with pictures from over the years. I bet there are some of your Mama in this room when she was your age. And the whole family."

This is my family home. My mom grew up here.

What did Mom call it– *my legacy.*

Then a bell rings. "What's that?" I ask.

"Rian, that bell means it's time for mint juleps and sweet tea on the back porch. It's a long standing tradition your great, great grandaddy started. Can you run out to the shop and tell Travis he best come in? I could call him on his cellular phone, but if he's got the music on, he won't answer. That boy could live under the hood of a car." Mrs. Day laughs. I stare at her. I mean, I don't work here. It's not my job to go get Travis. I'd much rather go down and have drinks with everyone else. She waves her hand to shoo me. "Well, what are you waiting for? Go on then, go fetch your cousin!"

"I... uh," I stammer. Who the hell does she think she is? She can't tell me what to do.

"Go on now, it's the last building before the tree line. You can't miss it." She points.

"You have lipstick on your teeth." I snip as I walk past her.

Outside the Benz and Range Rover have been moved. Darcy is gone, probably enjoying that mint julep and sweet tea Mrs. Day promised. I hear Mom's fake laugh trickling through the humid air. God, she's so annoying. I swat away the bugs as I walk. Why did I agree to do this again? Oh yeah, I didn't. Mrs. Day thinks she's the boss. But, give it a few weeks. I'll show her who's boss.

In Central Park you feel the presence of the city. You hear cars honking, you smell exhaust, you see the buildings over the tops of the trees. Not here. As soon as I reach the gravel path, heading toward Travis, I'm assaulted by vegetation; vines and plants growing every which way, ready to leap out and grab me. No city on the horizon to protect me. I kick the head off a flower and plot how I'm going to tell Mrs. Day she's got another thing coming if she thinks I'm going to start doing chores and errands for her.

That's when I hear the sound of metal clanking, coming from the last building before the treeline like Mrs. Day said. There is a huge orange and blue 76-Oil sign hanging on the side of the shop and car parts and pieces of machines laying around the yard. An old, broken down push mower is in a patch of grass where it probably died like a thousand years ago. This part of the property isn't well maintained and gives me the shivers. I don't belong way out here. This is so stupid. Mrs. Day can't force me to do anything I don't want to. What was

I thinking? I turn around and start the long walk back to the house.

"Not even gonna say hi to your long lost cousin?" A smooth, Southern drawl whispers behind me. I freeze. I didn't hear the crunch of gravel. The hair on the back of my neck stands and I suck in my breath. "Well, aren't ya gonna turn around?" he asks.

I slowly turn and standing there in greasy blue coveralls, his hair pushed back, stands Travis–looking like James Dean in *Rebel Without a Cause*. I slowly let out the breath I was holding. "Hey, Travis. Sorry, I thought maybe I was at the wrong place." I lie.

"Nope, this is it. My workshop. Wanna see the place?" He raises an eyebrow and half-smiles.

I shrug and follow him into the shop. There's a bright red muscle car with the hood up that looks like it cost a fortune. "Wow! Did you build this? It's really nice."

"No, this car was Daddy's. He was always tinkering on it and driving it up and down mainstreet every Sunday after church. It was off limits to me and Sam. But, with Daddy gone, I figure I better take care of it." Travis says mildly defensive.

He blinks a few times, like maybe he's trying to hold back tears. I can't help but notice his eyes are the clearest blue I've ever seen. If Ava was here right now she'd be going out of her mind. He's exactly the kind of boy she's not supposed to date. Her parents have already declared she's going to marry a "nice Jewish boy" from their Synagogue. Little do they know, if Ava comes here for Spring Break, she will try and take Travis and those baby blues home in her suitcase.

"Mrs. Day said you should come back to the house for sweet tea." I remember the reason for walking out here in the first place. I turn around to head back to the house, maybe I'll run and get the hell out of here. It's been such a long few days and I'm tired and honestly kind of irritated. Okay, a lot irritated.

"Hang on, I'll walk with you. Let me take this off quick," Travis shouts after me, but I don't slow down. Something about that car and this part of the property—the way Travis snuck up on me, it just gives me the creeps.

"Rian, wait up!" He catches up with me pretty easily. "I'm sure it's a big change. Leaving New York and moving out to the Everglades. Probably a lot of unfamiliar things. You doin okay?"

I don't know if it's the heat or the long drive, but something in me snaps. "If by doing okay you mean leaving my entire life behind, then yeah, Travis, I'm doing a-okay." I sound like such a brat.

"You know, you and Aunt Victoria didn't have to move here. I'll be eighteen soon, I can run things on my own," Travis replies and puffs up his chest.

"Oh really? What does that even mean, Travis?" I demand. My pulse pounds in my ears and my neck burns.

"It means you can go home." He folds his arms over his chest and lifts his chin.

"Really?" It comes out as an angry, forced laugh. "We can go home? And how are you going to afford any of this if me and Mom go home? Maybe if your loser dad hadn't murdered my Aunt and then killed himself, we wouldn't be in this mess."

Travis's face flushes bright red. "Sorry to inconvenience you, Rian," he growls.

"Yeah, actually, this is an inconvenience! I missed the last day of school and all the parties with my friends!" Like he would ever understand.

"I'll make sure to let Mama and Daddy know when I visit their graves, they put a damper on your New York socialite schedule." He runs for the house, leaving me standing alone, feeling more stupid than I already do.

"YEAH WELL FUCK YOU TOO!" I shout, letting my nasty temper get the better of me. But Travis is long gone. I look around, slightly embarrassed. Mom warned me to be on my best behavior.

"That went well," says a gruff voice. I spin around. Standing behind me is the biggest man I've ever seen in my entire life, smiling a big toothy grin through a beard and dabbing his bald head with a rag.

"Mind your own business," I tell him.

"They said you were sassy." The man laughs. He's wearing a pair of dirty blue coveralls like Travis was wearing. I didn't realize there had been someone else in the garage.

"Excuse you?" My face wrinkles up.

"My name is Jackie. Well, Big Jackie is what everyone calls me. I work here. Seen a lot over the years, but not too many folks can piss off your cousin Travis like that." He rubs the sweat off his huge egg-shaped head again.

"AND?"

"Well, I'm just sayin little miss, you were pretty hard on him. He's been through a lot and it's a big responsibility takin over this place." The sun glints off his scalp and he stares at me with brown puppy dog eyes, like he's trying to make me understand his point. "People don't always take kindly to strangers."

I stomp my foot. "We aren't strangers! My mom is Travis and Sam's legal guardian. It's her job to look after them and whatever dumb business my Aunt and Uncle had going on here." I can't believe I have to state the obvious.

"Dumb business... I ain't never heard no one call the company that before." He scratches his beard.

"What were they anyway? Cabbage farmers?" I say as snotty as I can before turning to walk back to the house. I don't need to play twenty questions with this unusually large man. But he easily keeps up. God his legs are as tall as me.

"Don't you know? Your Aunt and Uncle were some of the richest folks in South Florida! They inherited your Gramps fishing lure empire and all of your Gram Tweety's land after your Mama ran off to New York," he exclaims.

My mind is reeling. No pun intended.

Fishing lures?

Richest folks in South Florida?

This man is off his country rocker.

"Like I care," I respond and run for the front door. I storm up the stairs and into my room. I take out my phone and call Ava. I pretend everything is great and listen to her talk about the last day of school, but she has to go after a few minutes. Her and Maggie and Gina are going dancing at some new club.

I throw myself onto the bed and stare at the ceiling for a while. Finally, I pull out my sketch pad and new graphite pencil set. The set came in the mail from Germany a few days before we left home. No card from Dad. No well wishes. But, it's the thought that counts, right? I open the familiar pages of my favorite leather bound pad and start a new drawing of New York City being overgrown and choked out by vines and finally I add in an overlay of flames, burning everything to the ground.

Because that's what it feels like Cullier Manor House is going to do to me.

"Rian, you want to come down and have dinner?" Mom knocks on the door.

"No. I'm tired."

And overwhelmed.

9

JUST BE YOURSELF

MUSIC PLAYS SOFTLY FROM my phone while I'm soaking in the clawfoot tub the next morning. Mrs. Day was right. She did fill the drawers up with all my favorites. Costa Brazil bath salts, Verb shampoo, and even an Oribe lotion set.

I woke up at five because I heard voices whispering outside my room. But, when I went to look there was no one there. The house was quiet; everyone was still sleeping. I tip-toed around and explored. In the great room, on the main floor, I carefully picked up various antiques and looked them over. Not snooping! I'm into vintage stuff, remember? In the kitchen, I took a blueberry muffin from under a glass dome before going back to my bed. I lounged for a while and sketched a few new pictures that were less dramatic than what I drew last night before deciding to soak in the tub.

As soon as I'm done, I'm going to find Mom and demand answers. I am old enough to know what the hell is really going on here. I mean, she's the one talking about hiring Darcy and the business and all that. Then, that big man told me my Aunt Kris and Uncle Chuck owned some fishing lure empire. Why doesn't Mom just sell all of it and we can move back home to New York and take Sam and Travis. Just put this place behind us.

"Rian?" Mom calls from outside the bathroom door as I'm getting dressed. "Can I come in?" she asks gently.

"Fine." Now's my opportunity.

The door creaks open. "Oh, Rian! You look fabulous in those colors."

I'm wearing the sundress she bought me from Dolce & Gabbana before we left. I hate how it looks on me, but her face melts when she sees me. "The green and blue bring out your eyes. You're gonna blossom here in the south, I just know it," she says confidently. But, to me, it sounds completely condescending.

"Really?" I reply and shoot her a nasty look as she leans against the countertop. She's still in her pajamas. Pink silk. I've never seen them before. God, she's corny.

"Look, I know this must feel pretty overwhelming. But I promise it's going to be good for us. I want you to know I completely understand it will take time for you to get used to life at Cullier Manor House. My plan is to spend the summer getting things with the business sorted out so this fall I can focus on helping you and your cousins get through high school and into college–" she pauses.

I take her pause for granted and jump in before she can finish. "Were you ever going to tell me? A massive fishing lure empire? Jesus, Mom! I mean, that's kind of a big deal." I walk back into the room to find my other make-up bag. Mom's mouth is open when I walk back in, like she's ready to say something else. But I go right back at her, "And how do you think Sam and Travis feel? We just swoop in and you take over what their parents meant to leave to them? Can't you just sell it all and give them their cut and take us home to New York?" I lean into the mirror to put on my mascara.

"Rian, I'm not surprised, but I am hurt. I love Sam and Travis. They are my nephews. I know on the surface you think I had cut all ties with my roots. That's what your Dad needed to believe." Mom takes a big breath, her chest heaving. I look at her sideways. "The truth is, I spoke with your Aunt Kris on a regular basis. She was my only sister and I loved her very much. I never intended to be away from home as long as I was, especially after our parents died."

"Right, blame Dad. Like usual. He never stopped you from having a relationship with your sister." I stare at her. She looks vulnerable and sad with dark circles under her eyes and wrinkles around the edges of her mouth. Her hair is flat and lifeless. God, I wish she'd go shower and put her make-up on.

"Oh sure, side with him again. How predictable, Rian." Mom rolls her eyes.

"You can leave now," I tell her.

"No, I can't. We have to sort this out so you can grow here." She folds her arms over her chest.

"Grow here? Like I'm one of the flowers out in the yard? Nice, Mom. But seriously, as soon as I'm eighteen, I'm heading right back to New York. This place will never be my home. Travis and Sam hate me. I feel so out of place."

"You've been here for less than twenty-four hours, Rian. You don't know if you're out of place or not and your cousins don't hate you. They are desperate for you to be their friend. They were so excited to get to know you yesterday and you had to ruin it with your tantrums and skipping dinner." She closes her eyes and sighs. "Those boys just lost their parents in the most disgusting way. They need family and love, not your bad attitude."

"FINE."

"Fine what, young lady?" Mom narrows her gaze at me.

"Fine, I'll get to know Sam and Travis and be nice. But, I want to go back to New York for school shopping and to see my *real friends*," I demand.

Mom shakes her head no. "To be honest, Rian, Uncle Chuck was up to some shady business dealings before he died, and it's going to take me and Darcy months to get things straightened out. But, I plan on taking you and the boys to New York for holiday shopping and to see the Christmas Tree at Rockefeller Center. There's no way we can go any sooner."

No New York until the Holidays? That is ludicrous!

"And if you're nervous about your cousins liking you, just be yourself. When you aren't so concerned about being a NYP— you're a pretty great person." She walks out of the bathroom and shuts the door before I can argue. I slam my mascara on the counter. My favorite not-so-passive aggressive move.

"Mrs. Day, what's the WIFI password?" I ask the house-keeper a little later in the kitchen. She's busy bossing the cooks around. Why are they making so much food? Do they feed all the people who work here? I realized just how many people work here when I took a walk around the grounds after my argument with Mom. I had to clear my head. Kind of hard to do when every ten steps someone is saying "Hello!" and "Welcome home!"

"WIFI? What's that dear?" she asks without turning to look. She's dipping a wooden spoon into some white gravy looking stuff on the stove and tasting it. She adds some salt to the dismay of the cook and tries it again with the same spoon. Gross.

"Nevermind. Where's Sam?" I ask. He will know.

"Oh honey, Sam and Travis packed a cooler and head-ed for the skiff hours ago. They said they needed to go fishing and feel the sun on their shoulders. Those boys are something, ain't they?" she says with a twinkle in her eye.

"But my phone hardly works here. I need Sam to give me the WIFI password," I complain.

"Well, why don't you have Big Jackie take you in the side-by-side to the swamp dock and see if you can flag down the boys. You should go fishing. Might do you some good. Those little phones will make you go cross-eyed anyway."

"Um, no thank you. I don't fish."

"Oh dear, you better learn if you want to fit into the Everglades. We all enjoy the serenity of a day in the swamp catching dinner." She starts humming and walks around with a dish rag, pushing crumbs into her hand and throwing them in the sink.

"Ewe. I am not eating swamp fish. Don't be disgusting, Mrs. Day."

Mrs. Day and the cooks burst out laughing.

"Then you're gonna be hungry tonight, cause swamp fish is on the menu!"

"Bleh!" I gag. And that causes more laughter. I want to tell them to shut their ugly mouths. But, Mom's voice in my head. *Use your manners, Rian. Be nice to these people.* "I'll figure out the WIFI on my own."

I march down the hallway and look for any signs of a desk or someplace where there would be a password written on a sticky note. Mrs. Day mentioned she had an Apple computer someplace around here. There's a door open to a room I haven't snooped in yet. It's a library with shelves all the way up to the ceiling. I wander around and it's impressive. I'm half-tempted to take one of the books. But, oh no! I take a big step back and shake my head. I am not turning into some lame teenager with a #summerreadinglist or something stupid like that. I look around, but there's no password I can find, so I slump into one of the oversized leather chairs and debate my aversion to summer reading. Just as I'm about to get up and see if there are any steamy romance novels on the shelves, I hear my name.

"Rian," Darcy calls for me in the hallway.

"I'm in the library," I shout.

Darcy opens the door, following my voice. She looks around, joy on her face, as she takes in the grandeur of the private collection. Of course Darcy is a book nerd. I roll my eyes.

"Funny finding you in here," she says. Thank god I didn't get up and take a book off the shelf–I'd never hear the end of it from Darcy. She'd have me in a book club before the end of the day.

"Don't get any ideas about me and books. I was only in here looking for the WIFI password."

"When I was your age I couldn't stop reading–" but before she can tell me what horrible novels she read when she was a brace-faced teen back in Illinois, I put my hand up.

"What do you want?"

She huffs a little. As if she thought she'd finally found a way to bond with me– over books. Yeah right, Darcy.

"I just came to tell you Mrs. Day said the boys are out fishing and suggested you should join them," she says and smiles, a little smirk on her face.

"Are you serious?"

"Like Florida heat." She laughs at her own joke.

"Funny. But seriously, Darcy. Can I talk to you about something, other than books and fishing?" I ask.

"Of course, Rian. You can always talk to me," she says and takes a seat in the leather armchair across from me.

"Why did my Dad always imply Mom grew up like poor white trash? I don't understand any of this."

"Well, I don't know your dad all that well. He wasn't around much," Darcy answers my question with a non-answer.

"Bullshit!" I yell.

"Excuse me?" She gasps and leans back in her chair.

"You and mom spent like the last five years together," I remind her. God, why is Darcy being so dense.

"Um, yeah, Rian. Me and your MOM. All the times I'd be at your house, where was your Dad?" She narrows her gaze on me. I think about it. I guess Dad did spend most of his time in his stupid office. Or on the phone. Or gone. Now that I think about it, did Dad ever talk to Darcy?

"Oh yeah, I guess he wasn't around much," I finally admit.

She nods with agreement and angles her body forward. Then in a husky voice, she says, "If you want my opinion, I think your Dad had a certain image he liked your Mom to portray." She looks around nervously. "I think he was scared of this place. Like people might accuse him of things, you know, being married to a woman who was raised on a southern farm. Even one in the Everglades that made fishing lures."

The skin between my eyebrows wrinkles together.

"Now, this is only my opinion, but I think your mom went along with it because she loved your dad. She tried for a long time to be the perfect, New York woman."

I use my thumb to smooth out the frown between my brows, then massage my temples trying to make sense of it. "But, why would dad do that? Why make mom be someone she really wasn't?"

"Rian, honey, there's a lot of stuff you don't need to worry about. Adult relationships are sticky and complicated. All you need to worry about is getting along with your cousins and trying to have some fun this summer." She sounds just like Mom. "Look, your mom and I have a lot to do the next few days and then I've got to fly back to New York for a week. Would you please, for me, just try to be nice?"

"Whatever, Darcy," I say and fold my arms over my chest. "And teenage relationships these days are a lot messier than you might think. But, I'd never make someone I cared about disown their family and be someone they're not."

"I know you wouldn't, Rian." Darcy's compliment surprises me. "Now, get your New York butt outside and enjoy the sunshine!"

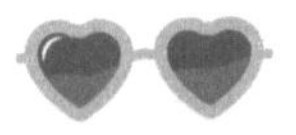

10

Mud, Mud, Everywhere

THE HEAT IN THE Everglades is unbearable. I'm slick with sweat the second I step out of the front door and onto the porch. The first thing I notice, besides the heat, is how loud it is. Not like New York loud. Not taxis honking and the hum of buildings and the sounds of people shouting loud. But, the ever present buzzing of insects and the sound of a chainsaw in the distance. A shovel punching into dirt in the garden. The water in the fountain. Someone whistling. A door slams. And there is a loud thumping from around the side of the house. I can't figure out what it could be. So, I walk that way to investigate.

When I come around the corner, past a pink and orange flowering shrub, I see the man from yesterday. Big Jackie. He's the one making the noise. Him and some girl are using huge, metal rakes and beating a rug hanging on a line. They are arguing fiercely about something, but I can't hear what they are saying over all the slamming and whomping sounds. The girl drops her rake and marches up to Big Jackie. She is waving her arms and pointing her finger, and for a moment, I think she's going to push him.

He put his rake down and his head too.

I grabbed my sketch pad before coming outside. There's a spot near a tree with some shade and a little cement bench. I'm not sure it's meant for people. It looks like garden art. But, I am not sitting down on the dirt in my Dolce&Gabbana. By the time I reach the bench, they've stopped arguing, but I can tell whatever it was about is eating her alive.

She's tense.

I watch as they remove the rug and put a different one up over the line and start working on it. I sketch her. She has lean shoulders. She's wearing super short jean shorts with frayed edges that hug her in the right spots. I look down and make a stroke with my pencil, then back up at her. I can't take my eyes off of her.

Finally, when the sweat drips from my forehead onto my paper, I decide maybe I will find Travis and Sam on the boat. I bet it's cooler on the water. So, I get up and walk toward Big Jackie and the mystery girl and wave to catch their attention. Big Jackie stops and wipes the sweat from his brow.

"Hey there, Miss Rian. You ever seen rugs cleaned this way in the Big Apple?" He laughs as he says it like it's the most ridiculous thing he's ever said to someone. I smile, only because his laughter makes his whole body shake.

"No, I guess I've never seen that before." I shrug. "I think they use vacuum cleaners in New York."

Big Jackie and the mystery girl both laugh—which is kind of annoying. Like, are they laughing at me?

"Rian, this is Justine. She's my little sister. Justine, this here is Rian," Big Jackie introduces.

Justine is half of Big Jackie's size. I don't see any resemblance. Big Jackie is bald and like ten feet tall and in his thirties. He's red and sunburned and sweaty from working outside all the time. And he's got a huge, grizzly beard that's red now, but when he gets old and gray I'm sure he will look just like Santa Claus. But Justine, she looks my age. She's got sunkissed hair, the kind you pay five-hundred dollars for, but hers is probably natural. Her skin, it's not all red and splotchy like her big brother's. She must use sunscreen. Her lips are perfectly moisturized and a little pouty, my heart skips a beat awkwardly.

"Hi, Justine."

"Hey, Rian. I like your dress," she says. There's a glimmer in her eye as she looks me up and down, doing her own assessment.

"Thanks, it's from the latest Dolce collection," I reply, hoping to impress her.

"I got one kinda like it from the Bealls Outlet store. You ever been? They got all kinds of fancy stuff from department stores that go outta business," she explains.

Outlet store? Oh god. But all I say is, "Oh yeah?"

"There's one about thirty miles away. If you like bargain shopping," Justine adds, "I could take you sometime."

If I laugh she will think I'm a spoiled, rich bitch. But seriously, bargain shopping? I might think she's cute, but no amount of flirting could take away from how awkward it would be. Her holding up a cheap dress and telling me I'd look good in it? I'd buy it to be nice and then burn it later. When she asked why I'd have to admit I don't wear mixed polyester blends from China. Then it would be like this big argument and she'd tell me what an asshole I am and I'd tell her how stupid her pretty face is. I know me, I know I can't be fake.

"Shopping, yeah maybe," I whisper. Better to say as little as possible. I'm supposed to be trying to fit in. It's better if I just walk away. "Nice to meet you." I turn and head back toward the house.

"Hold up, little missy!" Big Jackie comes after me. Justine isn't far behind.

"I'm hot," I say and don't stop walking.

"Well, hold up now. You want me to take you out to the boys? It's cooler on the water." Big Jackie wipes more sweat off his face. The sun is beating down so hard I'm going to faint.

"I don't know." I hesitate. But the thought of being near water sounds glorious. "Um, do you know what a side-by-side is?" I ask, remembering Mrs. Day said to ask for a ride on one. Then to my surprise, Justine starts laughing. She looks at her brother and back at me and doubles over. Tears pour from her eyes like I'm some clown with a big, red nose. Like really? Who the hell does this girl think she is laughing at *me* like that.

"Justine, don't be so rude," Big Jackie exclaims.

"Did I say something funny?" I put my hands on my hips.

Big Jackie's eyes dart around nervously and he speaks for his sister. The bitch. "No, little missy, just–well, a side-by-side is an ATV. See that thing over there? Like a golf cart with big wheels for going in the mud and driving around the property. Everyone's got one round here." He points toward a vehicle parked next to one of the outbuildings. Justine has finally stopped laughing.

"What's a side-by-side? Oh, Rian, that's good. I haven't laughed like that in a while, thank you, serious-ly–I needed that." Justine walks away and toward one of the small houses that dots the property.

Steam comes from my ears. "Take me to Sam and Travis," I say through gritted teeth and make my way to the hillbilly vehicle. Big Jackie follows after me.

"You sure you want to wear that fancy dress out to find your cousins? It might get muddy. I can take you back to the house to change," he offers.

"Muddy?" I ask.

He nods and drives us slowly over to the front of the Big House. "Go on now, put on something you can get dirty." I get out and walk up to the door. I've still got my sketchbook in my hands. But, I know me, if I go inside and feel that cold air conditioning, I won't come out again. So, I put my sketchbook down on the porch and climb back in next to Big Jackie.

"It's fine. Just go."

"Uh, you sure?" he questions. But, all I want now is to get out of here and find my cousins. I'm still fuming over Justine laughing at me.

"I said it's fine. GO!" I yell.

"Buckle up," Big Jackie grunts and steps on the gas as soon as I'm strapped in.

I expect a golf cart ride. I've been on them before, not too bad, kind of fun actually. But what I get is a forty-mile an hour, wind-in-my-face, bugs slapping me, eyelids flapping, screaming bloody murder ride.

"JACKIE!" I scream and squeal.

But, he laughs and does a figure-eight out in the middle of a swampy field, mud and water flying up around us in a huge sheet. He manages to whip the side-by-side over and the mud sheet sloshes inches from me. He keeps pushing further out into the fields and swamps before stopping at the edge of a dock that heads out into a waterway. Giant oak and palm trees are everywhere along the water, and tall grasses. I'm wet and muddy. My dress is ruined. But, that ride made me feel alive. My heart pounds.

"Sorry, I guess I got carried away," Big Jackie says when he realizes how filthy I am.

"I should have changed. It's my own fault." I unbuckle and jump out.

"Justine can wash your dress," he offers.

But, I already know it's ruined. I just shake my head.

"Where's Sam and Travis?" I ask and walk down the wooden plank dock. I look left and right and don't see a boat anywhere. I sit down on the edge since my dress is trash already, it doesn't really matter now. I lean over and get some water and splash my arms to get the mud off. I let my toes dangle. The water is cool and feels like heaven.

"Be careful. That water's filled with gators." Big Jackie comes up behind me.

I scream and pull back. I look at him horrified. Gators? And I had my hands and feet in that water! Before I can get pissed off, Big Jackie puts his hands up to his mouth and starts making some god awful sound.

"SKEESKOOO!" It's like a cross between a scream and a bird call. He does it three times before out in the distance we hear a similar sound in return.

"The boys. You just wait here for 'em."

"Okay well, thanks for bringing me out here," I say and hold my hand up to block the sun from my eyes.

The swamp water sparkles and reflects the light back at me. This entire place is so bright. I wish I had my Versace sunglasses. And bug spray. I slap a mosquito sucking my arm, a spot where I washed the mud off. My other arm is totally fine. Maybe I should have left the mud. "Do you have bug spray?" I ask Big Jackie, but he's already walking away.

Gnats fly around my face and I swat at them. I lean over the dock and stare into the water–my reflection looking at me with a smirk. I wonder how many gators are actually in the water and if they really are brave enough to swim up and bite a person with their toes in. After a few minutes I stand and put my hands on my hips and look out through the tall, swamp grasses, scanning for any signs of my cousins. That's when my eye catches the edge of a silver boat coming around the corner. Sam waves and has a grin from ear to ear. Travis is driving and even from here I can see he has a scowl on his face.

"RIAN!" Sam shouts. "Whoa girl, looks like you been muddin." He laughs when the boat gets up to the dock and he sees the state of my dress.

"Yeah, Mrs. Day told me to have Big Jackie bring me here in the side-by-side. I didn't know what that meant until it was too late." Explaining the mud.

"There's not a Chanel for hundreds of miles. You gonna survive, cous?" Travis asks. I take Sam's outstretched hand and get into the boat.

"That's not gonna work on me Travis. Sam was wearing Lacoste yesterday. You both wear Apple watches. And from what I hear, you're loaded. I might be from New York, so I don't know about all this country stuff, but I'm not stupid. Now, let's get out on the water. I'm hot." I plunk down on the seat of the boat. There's a pair of rainbow coated sunglasses in the cupholder and I put them on. "Do you have any music on this boat? Maybe a bottle of water too?" I snip. "Oh and this is Dolce&Gabbana not Chanel. Get it right next time you want to insult me."

"Ha, ha, Rian!" Sam laughs and hands me a bottle of water out of the cooler. "Bro, she nailed you. Chanel? Really?"

"Shut up dick." Travis pushes down on the accelerator and we careen out into the swamp. He zig-zags between big clumps of grass and reeds, like he could do this with his eyes closed. I'm holding on for dear life trying not to scream.

Finally we get to whatever spot in the swamp Travis thinks is good for fishing. He stops the boat, turns on the radio, and whistles along with the music. He pulls out his fishing pole and goes to work with the lure. I see the care he's taking. I am actually interested in it. That must be one of the lures that has made him and Sam the wealthiest teens in the Everglades. I don't know anything about fishing lures, but I can tell it's special. The shape and colors make it look like a real fish. Travis glances at me and I blush and turn away.

Sam's busy casting and setting his pole up in some kind of metal thing that holds it for him. He gets out another fishing pole and hands it to me. "Rian, y'all ever go fishing up in New York?" he asks in his sweet southern drawl.

"Not really. Not like this." I remember that time Mom took me to Central Park to go fishing when I was eleven. She entered me in a Youth Fishing Derby. But it was so gross. I cried when they made me put a worm on the hook and Mom took me home before it was over. "Mom took me to Central Park and we tried to go fishing once." I tell a half-truth so I don't seem completely foreign to them.

"That's awesome. Fishing in Central Park, now that sounds like something I could get used to doing in the city." Sam actually sounds impressed.

Travis just makes some grunt sound.

"What?" I ask.

"Figures," Travis says.

"What figures, Travis?" I fold my arms.

Sam gets quiet and acts like putting bait on the end of my pole is the most interesting thing in the world. I should be paying attention to what Sam is doing, so I can learn how, but I'm too busy glaring at Travis from behind the rainbow glazed plastic sunglasses.

"Nothing," he mumbles and casts his line in a perfect swoop. The shiny green and gold lure plops into the water. There is no denying he's been doing this his entire life. It looks effortless and relaxing, even when I see how tense his neck and shoulders are.

"Humphhhhh," I make a noise and turn back toward Sam.

Two can play at this game.

"Saaaaaam," I whine in my cute girl voice. "Can you please help me? How do I make the end go out into the water?" I hold out the pole to him. If I can't get Travis to just admit whatever shit is on his mind, I'll turn Sam into my new BFF and drive Travis mad until he breaks. Boys are so easy. This is a game the NYP's play back home.

"Okay come here. See this part, this is the reel. It holds the finishing line. Right here, this metal part, when you push it down you have to hold your finger like this," he says as he moves my hand on the line and flips open the metal thingy. I'm not sure I understand, but I just do what he says and he seems to approve and keeps going.

"Like this?" I say oh-so-sweetly.

"Great! You're a natural!" he laughs. I hear Travis make another grunt.

"Now what? I throw it into the water and catch a fish? Like a salmon?" I ask.

Before I have time to react, both Sam and Travis burst out laughing. My face feels instantly hot. I look back and forth between them. They hoot and cluck like a couple of chickens.

"Oh, Rian." Sam quits laughing.

"Girl, you can't be serious," Travis says. His shoulders are finally relaxed. "We don't have salmon out here in the swamp."

"Well how the hell am I supposed to know what kind of fucking fish are in the Florida swamps? GOD!" I have completely lost my cool.

"Chill. It was funny. Salmon are cold water fish. They live in the ocean and rivers up near Alaska. We catch Bluegill, Bass, and Catfish out here. All good for fryin up in a pan." Travis smiles. It suits him, looking happy, talking about the types of fish in the swamp. Just like yesterday at the garage. He looked happy then, talking about cars and his dad. Until I ruined it. Maybe I shouldn't have been such a bitch. I hate when Mom is right.

"Hey, sorry for yesterday, if I made you mad. Sometimes I have a bad attitude," I admit to him. He shades his eyes from the sun and nods.

"I'm sorry too. I know it was a big move, and coming here probably ain't easy when you had a good life back in New York," he says and I can tell he means it.

"Woah, Rian, you got company!" Sam shouts.

I look back and see that my fishing pole is bouncing around. I had set it down, I guess I didn't know the line dropped in the water. But it's tugging up and down, like something is on the end.

"What should I do?" I scream.

"Grab it before it goes over the edge," Travis shouts.

I jump for the pole which starts to get dragged over the side of the boat. My foot catches on the seat and I tumble forward, my hand grasping the slim pole. The boat rocks from the sudden movement and I flap my other arm to try and catch myself, but there's nothing to hold onto. I'm airborne before I know what's happening and going over the edge. All I can do is imagine being eaten alive by swamp alligators.

"RIAN!" Sam and Travis yell at the same time.

They grab ahold of my body and tug and we all topple backward onto the floor of the boat in an awkward pile of teenage flesh. There's arms and legs turned this way and that. But somehow, my fist is still clasped tightly around my prize.

"I didn't drop it, I still have the fishing pole," I exclaim and hold the pole in the air like a wand. I grasp the pole with both hands now, and the clear fishing line is jerking and tugging like a live wire in the wind. Whatever is on the other end of it is mad. I try to get up, but I can't.

"Hold on tight, cous, you gotta reel it in," Sam shouts from the bottom of the pile.

"How?" I whine.

"Turn the handle," Travis says and tries to put his hand up to help.

"Watch it, that's not the handle," I shriek and laugh. I grab the little black plastic knob on the reel, and turn. It makes a clicking sound as the line winds up. I'm trying my hardest to reel it in fast, but we are still piled in the bottom of the boat which makes it extremely difficult. I'm about to give up when I feel a change. The pressure isn't so much on the line, but like the fish is getting close to the surface of the water. I pull the pole back with one quick jerk.

"NO!" Sam and Travis shout. They scramble and try to get out of the way, but none of us can move, there is literally nowhere to go. A huge, green fish comes flying right at us on the end of my line.

I scream and then we are all laughing hysterically and squirming and pushing and shoving to get up and out of the way of the slimy fish that has landed in my lap. I'm crying, I'm laughing so hard. Somehow the boys manage to get untangled and jump up. Travis extends a hand to help me. Sam has plucked up the fish and my pole.

"That was like something from a movie," I say. I push my hair out of my eyes and wipe my face with my arm. I am so sticky and wet.

Travis takes one hard look at me with those crystal blue eyes. "We better get you back to clean up before supper or Aunt Tori might have a conniption fit if she sees you! Quit rubbing your face, Rian. You've got swamp mud every which way to Sunday," he says and points to the seat next to him. So I sit.

"That was a whole lot of southern packed into one statement," I tease.

Travis nods. "Yes ma'am!" And with that, he turns on the motor and we roar through the swampy waterways and I can't say I'm happy about the state of my clothes, or apparently my face, but I am happy about the time I spent with Sam and Travis. I guess I kind of like them. I mean, they are sort of fun and make me laugh.

Maybe, just maybe, being here won't be so bad after-all.

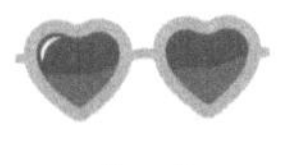

11

GHOSTS IN THE DARK

"HEY, RIAN," SAM HISSES. He's outside of my bedroom door.

"What," I say. He doesn't respond. "Sam, what is it? I'm awake, you can come in." The door opens slowly. Sam looks like he's just seen a ghost. I check my phone. It's almost 2 a.m. I'm only awake because I was sketching and group texting with Ava, Gina, and Maggie. They were telling me all the gossip from back home.

"I can't sleep." He comes in and sits on the foot of my bed.

"And you think I can help you with that?" I ask.

"No, but I thought maybe you'd want to go and hang out in the blind with me and watch for critters," he suggests. I narrow my eyes on him. He's wearing camouflage.

"Why would you ever think I'd want to do that?"

"Well, you come from a city that never sleeps. So you might like to see how alive the Everglades are at night. Lots of things don't sleep round here. But, maybe I thought wrong." He gets up and heads for the door.

"Wait, can I ask you something?" I set my sketchbook and pencils to the side and sit up, pulling my knees to my chest, and resting my chin.

He turns around and nods.

"Why'd it look like you saw a ghost when you walked in here?"

He smiles before answering. "Because I did see one before I walked in. This place has all kinds of dead folks walking the halls at night." Then he wiggles his fingers and makes a ghost noise, like ooooooohhhh.

"Don't be stupid, Sam. And give me a second to change. I'll come with you to see the critters. But, do I have to call them that? Can I say animals?" He looks surprised. But, that's only because he doesn't know me very well. One thing these boys will learn is that I've got a wild streak in me. Plus, I can't stand my friends having fun without me. So no, I'm not letting Sam have an adventure in the middle of the night if I'm not there to participate.

"But critter just sounds so, critter-like," he teases me.

"You have such thick southern accents. I didn't know they had them in Florida." I point out while I'm looking for my shoes. What do you wear when you go outside at night in the Everglades anyway? I'm already wearing a baggy shirt, so I quickly pull on a pair of thin, black joggers over my pajama shorts and grab my favorite tie-died Bliss and Mischief sweatshirt.

"There are pockets all over Florida, especially up in the panhandle, with original settler families. We're the ones who still got thick accents. Least, that's what Mama said. Plus, Gramps came from Louisiana and my Daddy came from Alabama... so I guess we talk like them too."

I shrug. I guess that makes sense. I have my Dad's strong Connecticut accent, at least that's what Ava always tells me.

"You ready?" he asks impatiently.

"Yeah, what are you waiting for?" I ask.

Sam cocks his head at me and grins before leading the way out of my room. I peek around for any ghosts, but it's just me and Sam. There are candle-shaped LED lights in the hallway and down the stairs, the kind that flicker and mimic real candle flames. So, it's not as dark or scary as it could be. The entire house, I've decided, is vintage glam and I kind of love the aesthetic. Of course, I'll never tell Mom. She doesn't get the satisfaction of knowing I might actually like Cullier Manor House.

Sam doesn't sneak around. He just walks out the front door like he belongs here and here belongs to him. Which I guess it does. The house is so big no one will even hear or notice us leaving out the front door. For a moment I wonder how often my Mom and Aunt Kris snuck around because clearly it's pretty easy.

When we get out on the porch the summer night air is just as sticky and damp as it is during the daylight hours. I won't need my sweatshirt, but I carry it in my arms anyway.

"You remember when we were kids and played together on our one and only family vacation?" Sam asks as we walk along the path toward Travis's shop. There are solar lights dotted here and there in the gardens to illuminate the path.

"Yeah, I guess. My dad wasn't very happy on that trip. He sort of ruined it for me." Dad complained the entire vacation about my drunk Uncle Chuck.

"I thought you were so cool. Even for an eight year old, you were like this posh New Yorker," Sam tells me.

"I thought you were a big dork," I tease. "Country kids. With all your 'yes ma'ams' and 'y'alls'" I laugh. "But, look at you now, Sam. All grown up."

"I still say y'all and yes ma'am." He laughs too, pointing to a patch of trees off in the distance in a big field to the left of Travis's shop. "There. That's where the blind is."

"What exactly is a blind?" I ask. I try not to feel stupid like my earlier encounter with Justine and the side-by-side, or Mrs. Day and the fish, or come to think of it, all my encounters so far.

Sam is nice though and doesn't laugh at me. "It's like a tree house with camouflage on it. It lets us sit up high, hidden from the critters. They just go about their business and we can watch them. I've been trying to spot a Florida panther for my entire life. Mr. Jenkins said he's seen one hunting on his ground a few miles from here. They have huge territories spanning hundreds of miles. There are less than two hundred in the wild." His voice rings with excitement as he talks about the panther sighting. "I've had a hard time sleeping since my parents–" he pauses. "So, I come out here instead of sitting awake in my room all night."

"The panther, it can't eat us right?" I'm usually not scared of animals. I love going to the Zoo in Central

Park and watching the Tigers. But, they are in cages. A panther roaming free, that makes my heart palpitate.

"Course not! I won't let nothing bad happen to you, cous. I told Aunt Tori that I'd protect you," he says as we reach the base of the tree.

"Thanks, Sam. So, how do I get up in that thing?" I ask. We are under the tree he'd pointed at. He was right. It's like a big tree house. But, from where I can see there isn't any way to get inside of the tree house.

"There's a secret ladder. Travis hooked it up to voice command. We might be country folks, but we still use technology." He says with all seriousness. Oh, I can't wait for this!

He stands right below the tree house and then says into his Apple watch, "Lower the Ladder." And holy shit, some kind of trap door opens and a ladder comes down.

"Impressive!"

Sam smirks before he starts climbing. "Come on, before we scare the panther."

We would scare the panther? I highly doubt it. But, I don't wait for a second invitation. I climb up into the blind right after him. I have no idea what to expect when my head pops up into the small space. It's dark, but I imagine it's what a treehouse might be like. A little wooden room with small windows all the way around the edges and two small folding chairs to sit on.

Sam is already sitting on one of the chairs. I clamor in and sit on the other. "Now what?" I whisper.

"Now we wait," Sam replies. Then he hands me some funny looking sunglasses. I frown at them. But, I put them on anyway and suddenly I can see everything.

"Night vision," he says proudly. I don't mind him showing off all his hi-tech gadgets.

"Why is it all green?" I ask as I look around and watch things light up in the glasses.

"I think it has to do with the light luminescence that humans can see, the glasses enhance it. Animals have it naturally and can see in the dark, that's why they are so active at night. Okay Rian, see that space there, look through it." He helps me look out a spot in the blind after his quick science lesson. It looks pretty boring to me. Just the big open field with some clumps of grass and few shrubby palms.

We sit there for what seems like forever and it's so quiet.

I yawn. I'm about to take off my glasses, but there, oh my god. Something is moving.

"Sam, look." I point into the field. I'm seeing something prowling about in the grass and my blood pressure explodes, filling my ears with a thump. Could it be a panther?

"That's a skunk," he says softly.

"A SKUNK?" I shriek whisper.

"Shhhhhh!"

"But, won't we get sprayed?!"

Sam's only response is a muffled chuckle.

"I did not come out here to be sprayed by a skunk." I turn and glare at him. His face is distorted in the lenses of the night vision, and his eyes glow like the moon.

"Rian, we are up in the air. And that cute, little guy is at least twenty yards away, and on the ground."

Sam tries to reason with me. But, I'm mad. What if that skunk can climb a tree and decides to spray me? My skin and hair will be covered. This outfit would have to go in the trash. I'll have to cut all my hair off.

Fortunately, the skunk wanders away before I have a complete meltdown. We sit in silence for a while after the skunk sighting. He was right about the Everglades being awake at night. There are owls hooting. Cracks of branches in the woods. Other sounds I can't identify. The place is alive, that's for sure. I decide now's as good a time as any to ask Sam something that's been on my mind.

"Sam, what's the school like here?"

"It's fine, I guess. I mean, it's K-12. There's about fifty of us. I'm on the football team and baseball too," he says, still watching through the opening in the blind for the elusive Florida panther.

"Really? There's only fifty seniors?" I ask. Back home I had at least three-hundred people in my grade.

"No, like, fifty kids in the whole school," he says.

"Are you fucking kidding me?" I can't hide it. That's insane.

"You'll get to know everyone pretty quick," he replies. "There's eighteen girls in the high school. So you can be on any team or join any club you want, not a lot of competition. They are all excited for you to be here." He pauses and shifts in his seat, then he scratches his cheek, and wipes his hands on his pants– like his palms are sweaty. "I may have told everyone you were coming. I hope you aren't mad."

I hold my breath for a minute and think about what I'm going to say. "I'm not mad. But—" I know what I said back home in New York. That every girl would want to be me, or date me, but the more I think about it the more it scares me. "Maybe I'll just do online school."

"Online school?"

"Yeah, some of the best schools in the world are online," I explain. "Why don't you and Travis do online school or have a private tutor? Obviously your parents could afford it."

"Why would we do that?" He folds his arms across his chest. "We grew up here with all these folks, Rian. This is our home. This is your home now too."

"Yeah, sure Sam." Everyone wants me to say this place is my home, but I've only been here for forty-eight hours. I'm not ready to admit defeat and call this place anything other than a crappy summer vacation.

I'm just about to tell Sam I'm tired and we should go back to the house when I notice his body tense up. He's looking out at something in the field. Probably that awful skunk again. I swear if it takes one step closer to me, I'll freak out. But, Sam is slowly pulling some equipment from the bag by his feet. A camera. He doesn't say a word, he just pulls off a lens cover and aims out and takes pictures...

"Oh. My. God. That's a lion," I hiss.

"No, Rian. That's a Florida panther." His voice is so calm it verges on creepy.

I shiver.

I can hardly believe my eyes so I squint and blink fast, but the animal doesn't disappear. It's real and I can't take my eyes off the beautiful creature as it slinks slowly through the field.

"What's that next to it?" I ask.

"I'm not sure," he says and reaches for something else. He sets down the camera and puts up a pair of binoculars up to his eyes.

"Let me," I try to grab them. He just bats my hand away.

"Excuse you!" I say.

"SHHHhhhhhh!"

"Oh, you did not just shush me!" I whisper.

"Rian, Jesus, stop being so needy. Do you have any idea what we are witnessing?" he says. What an asshole! He slapped me away and now he has the nerve to tell me I'm being needy. I'm going to leave so fast he won't know what hit him.

"It's got a baby," he chokes the words out and hands me the binoculars just as I'm about to try and move this stupid ladder back down. I push them back.

"Liar. If they are so rare–"

"Just look!"

I snatch the binoculars and look out at the panther and the thing rustling around with it. Holy shit. Sam was right. That's a baby panther. And for fucks sake, it really is so cute. It's like seriously the cutest thing I've ever seen in my entire life.

"Simba," I whisper.

"Rian, you're witnessing history. Do you have any idea how special this is?"

Of course I don't. But I do know this is one of those moments that is better when someone is around to witness it.

"Will the kitten survive?" I ask and watch it chewing on a palm leaf. It's so adorable I can hardly stand it.

"I don't know. They are ultra endangered."

"Then we better enjoy this rare moment," I say, surprising myself. Hmm. See? I can be a good person if I want to be.

"Amen," Sam adds.

Sam and I sit in silence and watch the panther and her kitten for a long time. Sam quietly takes pictures with his night vision camera. The panther is sleek and smooth through the green lens of my night vision goggles. This experience is surreal and the more I stare at the panther, the more I feel connected to her. She's licking her kitten and nuzzling it with such care.

I lift my goggles just to see if I can see her without them, and she jerks her head up and looks at the blind. She stares right through the small window and makes direct eye contact with me. My instinct is to turn away and hide myself because I feel raw and bare and wide open to her. Predator and prey; she could run over here and climb up the tree if she wanted to. She could hold me down and dig her sharp teeth into my neck and rip me apart for daring to watch her and her child. She yowls and growls and purrs before finally winking at me, as if to say, *welcome home, Rian.* Then she nips at her kitten and together they wander off through the field, disappearing into the darkness like a pair of ghosts.

Wait...

Did she wink at me?

I rub my eyes.

"Sam, I think I'm seeing things. The panther, she winked at me," I yawn and lay my head down on his shoulder.

Sam gently pats my head. "Cous, that was incredible. I've spent years trying to catch a glimpse of a Florida panther. And to see one with a kitten–" he sighs. "I'm so glad you were the one here to see it with me."

I yawn again and nod my head up and down on his shoulder. "Me too."

"You know, Rian, this has been the worst few weeks of my life. I still can't believe my Mama is gone... But, with you and Aunt Tori here, it feels like maybe we can have a home again."

I swallow hard. I hate knowing how sad Sam has been. I mean– who can blame him. "Tell me about what she was like, your Mom." And he starts talking about her, the way she laughed, her constant list of projects around the house, the way she made pancakes on Saturday morning. It's nice to hear him talk about his mom. I close my eyes and paint a picture of what their life was like in my head. And Sam's words are the last thing I hear before I fall asleep.

I dream about the panther and her kitten.

They are chasing me. No, they are running next to me.

"Rian, you need to escape, you need to run away from the swamp, it's dangerous," Mother panther pleads.

I run harder and faster but I'm lost. I scramble and look around, searching for something to guide me until I see the bronze Alice and Wonderland statue in Central

Park on the East Side, a place I've been a thousand times. A place that I've sketched and used as inspiration for a hundred different drawings.

"Where are you?" I shout to mother panther.

But she's gone.

And I'm alone and it's cold.

God, why are dreams so annoying?

Eventually the sun starts peeking up over the far edge of the swamp and makes its way through the trees. The gentle warmth on my face wakes me. I'm disoriented. I expect to see the underside of the bronze mushroom. But, when I pull myself up, I'm not in Central Park, I'm in a hunting blind. Sam is sitting peacefully across from me, I'm not sure he ever slept. We climb down the ladder and head back to the house walking in silence. I feel like I was part of something special last night and if I say anything it will disappear. Sam must feel the same way, because he doesn't say a word either.

As soon as we cross the threshold of the house, he follows his nose to the kitchen, and I lug my tired body up the stairs to my room and crawl into my bed and fall asleep for half the day. I wake up feeling hungry and something else...

A strange feeling, something I wasn't expecting.

It's like a cross between excitement and appreciation. Like when you see all of the presents under the tree on Christmas morning. There's anticipation and happiness and magic wrapped up. Before I can dissect these new feelings any further, I smell something delicious wafting up from the kitchen. "Mmmm. Is that cinnamon?"

12

A MILLION ACRES?

EVERY MORNING FOR THE next week, I wake up bright eyed and throw off my crisp white sheets, excited for what the day might bring. As soon as my feet slide out of bed and hit the ground, I'm in a race to get dressed, brush my teeth and head outside to find Sam or Travis. Because hanging out with Mom while she works on her computer and talks on the phone about business license agreements and blah, blah, blah does not sound appealing to me. It sounds like torture.

So that means I've had a whole week of exploring Cullier Manor House and the property with my two cousins, who I've decided aren't so bad after all. They did save me from falling into the swamp our first time fishing. Not to mention the crazy night with Sam watching animals and hanging out in the tree blind.

They've shown me all eighteen buildings on the property, including two garages, Travis's workshop and an old 1790s barn. My head's been spinning with how big it is. I'm not sure I'll ever learn everything there is to know about this place... There are even secret passageways in the kitchen!

After grabbing a banana nut muffin from the kitchen and stepping outside, I lean up against the stone arch, trying to catch my breath. From getting ready so fast, and from the freaking heat. Now that's something I'm not sure I'll ever get used to. I eat my muffin, savoring every warm homemade bite, looking out at the big fountain in the middle of the driveway, watching as a flock of tiny birds swoop in and splash in the water. I'm about to walk over and see if I can get a better look at the little birds when I hear the ATV come flying around the corner of the yard. Sam and Travis are already covered in mud.

"Out early?" I ask and laugh.

"Did you know the Everglades is over a million acres," Travis says when I get into the ATV next to him after Sam hops in the back. I'm not into maps or anything, but I'm pretty sure a million acres is a lot bigger than Manhattan. "Yup. Everything west of Old Palmetto Drive is owned by our family."

"And apparently it's mostly mud and swamp." I reach a finger over and wipe a big chunk of gooey dark mud off his cheek and flick it.

"No, not all of it. There's a lot of farmland and trees too. It's practically a forest around here," he says and points to a cluster of palm trees in the distance. I laugh.

I remember the closest thing to a forest I'd ever been to in New York. "You know me and Ava tried walking around Central Park once. It's six miles all the way around. We only made it halfway before she called her driver to come get us."

Sam stifles a laugh and I turn around and smack his arm.

"You could walk all day and not reach the edge of our land," Travis says proudly. I hang on to the roll bar as he steps on the gas and we go skittering down the gravel driveway. We fly by the cluster of palm trees that seemed so far away only moments ago.

I look out over the land, and try to imagine walking for an entire day. I shake my head, he can't be serious. Can he? "So what are we doing today?" I lean over an yell over the growling engine.

"Huh?" Travis looks at me and puts his hand up to his ear.

"I said, *WHAT ARE WE DOING TODAY?*"

He slows down to a stop, near a twisted tree with low hanging branches, and turns off the ATV. "You don't have to shout."

I elbow him. He's such a smart ass! "Seriously, what are we going to explore today?"

Sam jumps out of the back, he's wearing long cargo pants, which makes me suspicious and he points into the trees. "You get to choose. If we go left, we can find the Native American ruins. If we go right, there's the wreck from Black Beard's pirate ship."

"Pirates?" I get out and put my hands on my hips, before swatting away the mosquitos. Oh shit, I forgot to put on bug spray. I'm going to hate myself tonight when I'm covered in red welts.

"You know what pirates are famous for, right?" Sam smirks.

"Killing? Looting? Raping women?" I'm not amused.

"No! Treasure. There's a secret buried treasure, some-where out there. Our family has been searching for it for years." Sam sounds like he really means it.

Before I can respond, Travis begs, "Oh come on Rian, it'll be fun, once we hack down the saw palmetto bushes with a machete, and climb through the vines, it's only a three or four mile hike."

"Excuse me? Machetes? Climbing? Hiking? I'm wear-ing $700 sandals and shorts." I roll my eyes and climb back into the ATV. "I think I'll stick to a peaceful drive today." I shake my head. First of all, I'm not a teenage detective on the hunt for buried treasure. And second, I'm not interested in ruining any more of my designer clothes.

"But aren't you bored with exploring and driving around the property yet?" Travis asks.

"There's so much to see, how could I be bored?" I think about my day yesterday. Sam and I drove on the ATV for three hours, stopping so I could sketch pictures of strange twisted trees while he demonstrated all the bird calls he could do with his hands. It was impressive.

"But there's so much more out there you haven't seen yet." Travis points into the wide unknown, then he lifts his cowboy hat and slicks back his hair.

Bzzzz...

"Agh!" I smack my neck. I'm being eaten alive. "Can we go now? I don't want to go looking for some stupid treasure." It's easy to slip back into my regular old self. "I just want to go back to the house and draw, is that okay?" The words come out of my mouth a lot harsher than I mean them to, but it does the job, Travis and Sam get into the ATV and we drive back to the big house without another word.

I slam the front door, thankful to be in the air-conditioned house.

"Rian? Honey is that you? Do you want to come have some tea with me?" Mom yells from the other room.

"NO!" I shout and stomp up the stairs to my room.

My weeklong high from seeing the Panther and her kitten was bound to come to an end. And apparently today was the day.

"Pirates? Treasure. What a load of shit." I kick off my shoes and throw myself onto the bed and pull my white sheets over my head. Maybe tomorrow I'll sleep in. I mean, what have I been thinking, waking up early? Going on adventures with my cousins? Like I'm going to stay here, like this is my home. It's not. And I can't forget that I'm a New Yorker. We don't go on swamp adventures.

13

BACKWOODS BARBIE

"RIAN! THAT'S A DOUBLE dribble."

"Shove it." I keep bouncing the ball. We are in the old hayloft of the barn. Which I learned is where the hay used to be stored on the second floor, back when they kept farm animals here. They don't have farm animals anymore—which I'm glad about. Do you know how smelly goats and cows are? Gross.

Sam and I are shooting baskets in a hoop that Gramps put up for Mom and Aunt Kris when they were kids. The wooden plank floors are uneven, which makes bouncing the ball harder than it should be. But I don't care, it's still fun.

"Foul!" He shouts when I push past him.

"What? You're just jealous of my sweet moves," I reply, spinning and twisting with the ball. I don't know what a double dribble is or a foul. I'm just happy I can bounce the ball at all. I've never been very good at sports. Sam runs forward and swipes the ball from me.

"No fair!" I shout and fold my arms over my chest. Then Travis surprises the hell out of both of us and rushes at Sam. He takes the ball easily from him, leaps up in the air and dunks.

"It's the boots, they give me wings." He laughs and kicks his cowboy boot heels together.

I let them fight over the ball and try to dunk on each other and I go climb onto the wooden swing that's on the highest rafter. Another one of Gramps installations. I wonder how often my mom sat in this very spot and who she watched playing ball. I'd ask her. But, she's off the property today. She left me a note this morning, she was heading to town to take a look at the manufacturing plant where they make the fishing lures. Of course she didn't even ask if I wanted to go and see the place.

I pull out my phone and turn on some music. I start singing along and pumping my legs on the swing. Sam and Travis don't say a word, which means, they don't think my voice is bad– or they are being polite.

It's freeing.

I would never ever, like never, sing in front of Ava or Maggie or Gina. We regularly laughed at people from our class who posted singing videos on TikTok and couldn't wait for the epic fails on American Idol. God, why were we such bitches?

I watch Sam and Travis for a while longer. But, it's getting hot in here and I need some fresh air. "I'm bored and hot," I whine.

"Let's go fishing," Travis suggests. So we all climb down the ladder.

"I need a few minutes to change," I tell the boys and head for the Big House. Today feels like a day for my red and white striped Valentino swimsuit. I love its vintage feel.

One thing I've discovered is that lazing in the sun is a totally acceptable way to spend the day at Cullier Manor House. If I told Sam and Travis I wanted to spend every day on the boat and they could fish, the answer would be a resounding yes. Mrs. Day would look like a peacock and tell me how proud of me she is, watching me spend time with my cousins and embracing the southern ways. After changing and getting a towel from my room I rush back downstairs. Now, where did I put my tanning oil and my little spray water fan? "Mrs. Day?" I push open the door to the kitchen, expecting to see her purple hair and lipstick teeth telling Mrs. Paula her meal plan for the week is terrible. (They seem to fight over the menu all the time). Instead it's someone I haven't seen since my first day here.

"She's gone." Justine looks up from her spot at the kitchen table. She's flipping through a magazine. She puts it down and takes a drink of her sweet tea. I recognize the cover. Last month's Vogue. Interesting.

"Hey Justine. I was looking for my tanning oil and fan. They aren't in my room. I thought maybe Mrs. Day put them somewhere." I glance around the table and counters. I don't see them anywhere.

Justine looks me up and down.

"You look good." Then she goes back to the magazine. "Use sunscreen. Keep that skin of yours from burning. I use SPF 50 everyday."

I open my mouth to say something, like mind your own business, I'll use tanning oil if I want too. But, then, wait, what was the first thing she said? I look good! I close my mouth. What does she mean by I look good? Like she thinks I look good, or she likes this swimsuit, or...

"RIAN, COME ON!" It's Travis out in the front hall.

"RELAX!" I scream back.

"You better go, the boys hate to be kept waiting." Justine has a smile on her face but she doesn't look up from the Vogue.

"Yeah, and I thought I was the spoiled one," I say. Justine laughs and the sound hits me in just the right spot and makes me long for more.

"Do you want to come out on the boat with us?" I ask her. This time she looks up. Her eyes glitter.

"I've got plans," she says. "But maybe another time."

"Well, you know where to find me." I let out a small nervous laugh before leaving the kitchen. I don't know what it is about Justine, she kind of infuriates me, but I also kind of want to get to know her better.

"I thought you said it would only take a few minutes?" Sam and Travis are waiting for me right outside the front porch with the ATV. I smile and jump in the back seat and buckle up. Justine strolls out and I watch her walk across the property. She looks over at me and I raise my hand to wave but Travis jerks the wheel and we go spinning around a stump so I have to hang on instead.

We spend the afternoon bobbing around in the water on the boat, soaking up sun and fishing. We talk and listen to music. I discover Sam's favorite subject, New

York. And for some reason, it doesn't hurt as bad talking about home, when I'm telling Sam while we are on the boat. He asks about everything. The architecture, the music, the art scene, the food.

"So you're tellin me, that they charge $25 for a piece of toast with an avocado on it?" Travis interjects when I'm telling Sam about my favorite restaurants and food.

"Yeah, I guess it's pretty stupid when you say it like that." I laugh. Then I tell them about the real NY cheesecake, acai bowls, sushi and oysters rockefeller. I tell them there is a bagel shop and hot dog stand on every corner. Not to mention all the pizza places.

"What about all the TV things?" Sam asks.

"What TV things?" I ask.

"You know, like that big Christmas tree or the ball dropping on New Years. You ever seen them?"

"Ohhh! Yeah, I've been to both." So I tell them about going to Time Square with Ava and Gina for New Years last year and drinking champagne and kissing some strange girl in the crowd when the ball dropped at midnight. Then I tell them about going ice skating at Rockefeller Plaza during Christmas break with Arthur Guinney and how he fell and broke his ankle and we had to sit under the Christmas tree and wait for the medics to come take him. All the tourists were yelling at us to get out of their stupid pictures. So me and Arthur started flipping them off, it kept him from crying in front of me and then I kissed him before he went to get a cast.

"Rian, can I ask you something?" Travis asks. He attaches a shiny green lure on his pole.

"Sure thing." I sit up from my slumped position in the seat, the boat isn't big enough to lay flat for suntanning, but I'm stretched as far out as I can.

"Do you date guys or girls? Not that it's my business, and I don't care. But, my friend Chase wanted to come hang, and—" Travis stumbles over his words. Then he drops the lure. "Shit." I slide my sunglasses up so I can get a better look at him. His cheeks are flushed and he lets out a long breath.

My sexuality was bound to come up sooner or later.

"And what?" I ask, when he doesn't finish what he was trying to say.

"And nothing. That was it. I texted a picture of you to Chase and he thought you were hot. But, you just talked about kissing a girl at New Years and then kissing some dude who broke his ankle." He won't look at me, instead he hyper focuses on getting the lure on the line. I smirk. I'm sure he never normally has this much trouble.

I laugh. "Yeah, I am pretty hot. I mean, I don't blame your friend Chase for wanting to meet me." I fake fan myself.

Travis's head snaps in my direction. "Better cool off there, cous. We wouldn't want you getting a big head." He leans over the edge of the boat and splashes water at me. I scream and reach over my side of the boat and splash him back.

"Seriously though, I'm not really into labels. I just like who I like. I guess the easiest way to explain it is that gender doesn't matter to me." I don't know if Travis will get it or not, but I am not going to hide who I am. I reach for my tanning oil, which I spot wedged between the seat and the metal cup holder. "Ah there you are," I say to ease the silence that has taken over. I put some on my legs but, after Justine's comment, I sort of wish I had sunscreen. I'll have to ask Mrs. Day if she can order me some.

"That's cool." Travis shrugs after a few minutes.

"Yeah, I can see that about you. You like what you like. Simple enough," Sam adds.

Phew! Thank god they aren't going to make it weird. Because I will not stay in Florida if I find out my cousins are phobic intolerant pricks. I'd walk back to New York on foot if I had to.

"So, you haven't told me. Who are you two dating? Seriously, are you ever going to bring your swamp girl-friends around to meet me?" I laugh.

Sam coughs and Travis turns around like he's hiding something and starts whistling.

"Uh, no no no. Just wait a second. What's that all about?" I sit up. "You seem up to something... Or wait, did I misread you both? Should I be asking when you're bringing your swamp boyfriends over to meet me?"

Sam splashes water at me this time from his seat on the front of the boat. Travis stops whistling and finally casts his line out into the water.

"Watch the hair!" I put my arms over my head.

"Neither of us is gay if that's what you're asking. Which is cool and all, but we are straight. It's just that Travis and his girlfriend broke up and he's still crying about it." Sam grabs his pole off the holder and starts reeling it in to check the line. "And I dunno, there ain't no one in town that I got my eye on right now." That disgusting southern charm. I'm sure he's broken a few hearts, maybe there's no one left to date in town...

But Travis? Crying about a girl. This oughta be good.

"Awe, poor Travie Wavie. Did a widdle southern belle break your heart?" I mock.

"Yeah and she was pregnant," Sam blurts out.

"Shut the fuck up man," Travis lunges forward at his brother. Like holy shit is he going to punch him?

"WHOA! STOP!" I put my hands out to stop them from fighting. My legs are slippery and when I leap up I slide forward. Travis grabs me around the waist and spins me back down into the seat.

Sam's face is priceless. "Jesus Rian, you've got to stop trying to fly off this boat."

"Yeah well you two country bumpkins better sit your asses down and dish the gossip. Travis, so you got a girl pregnant and dumped her? Or she dumped you?"

This is getting juicy! Travis looks like he still might knock out Sam. And Sam looks smug as hell. But, they are both sitting now and the noises of the swamp, the bugs and the water sloshing against the boat, are the perfect background for this southern fried drama.

"She," Sam starts again and Travis reaches forward with a fist. I'm half-up, half-down on the seat and realize this is actually serious. Travis is seriously pissed off and doesn't want me to know what happened. Or just really doesn't want to talk about it.

I better do something.

"Jesus Christ Travis. We are family! I just told you that I like guys AND girls. This is the Bible-Thumping-South! I could be stoned or some shit for admitting that. But, guess what, I AM WHO I AM. I WON'T APOLOGIZE for being ME. So, whatever happened between you and backwoods Barbie doesn't fucking matter. And it's not worth punching Sam over it."

"Well, damn Rian," Sam says and rubs his hand over his hair a few times.

"Yeah, damn," Travis adds. Then he takes a deep breath, sinks into his seat, grabs his fishing pole, and tells me all about Backwoods Barbie. He doesn't look at me when he talks, instead he stares out over the swamp water, gently reeling in his line and moving his fishing his pole up and down.

"Her name's Keri Lynn Casey."

Never trust anyone with three names. That's something Dad taught me.

According to Travis, Keri Lynn Casey and her family moved to town a few years ago, and she immediately weaseled her way into Travis' big ol' country heart. From his explanation, I immediately know the type. She's like the girls from Jersey. The ones who dress up and pretend to be New Yorkers, they come over in hoards across the George Washington Bridge. Me and Ava could spot them a mile away, the wannabees, the gold diggers, the fakes. Keri Lynn Casey is exactly like that.

"I mean, I knew she had issues, like all her lyin about stupid shit," Travis says. "But, I just figured she was tryin to impress me."

"She was a loser bro, remember that time after football practice and we saw her smokin weed with Levi and when you asked her she straight up lied and said she'd been out on the boat with her dad fishing all afternoon," Sam says. "She was always stoned or doing shady shit."

"Yeah I know man, she was a liar, but damn. You don't know what I'm going through, I thought I loved her. She made me feel special. And then she told me she was pregnant with my baby." He's quiet for a while and I look over when I hear him sniffle. He uses the back of his hand to wipe his nose. "I told her I'd marry her, but she fucking dumped me and her parents filed a lawsuit."

"Wait, what?" I gasp.

"Yeah," he mumbles. He reels in his line and adjusts the hook on the end of the lure.

"She said she was having your baby and then dumped you and her parents tried to cash in on the deal. Whoa… That is such a Jersey thing to do." I shake my head.

"I had to tell my parents. And Daddy, he about lost his mind. He wanted to settle it and pay her family off before anyone in town found out. Mama, she was all sentimental and wanted me to try and work it out with her." He casts the line back out and it plunks in the water. "But, I called Aunt Tori, cause I know she's a lawyer and all that. She helped me fill out the paperwork for something called an in-utero paternity test. And I signed some papers saying I wanted full-custody if the baby was mine. Cause I wasn't about to let a stoner raise my baby." Travis is sniffling again, this time I see tears on his cheeks. I bite my lip as hard as I can without it bleeding to keep myself from blurting out more profanities. If I ever meet Keri Lynn Casey, I'll smack her.

And mom. My mom. He called MY MOM for help, and she helped him.

"The test came back and the baby wasn't mine. She really was cheating on me. She really was just using me to get money. Do you know how shitty that feels," he moans. His head is in his hands. The tough guy Travis is nothing but a big ball of goo.

"What happened to Keri Lynn Casey?" I demand.

"Word got out in town, bout what she did. Everybody hated them after they found out and her family moved back home to Louisanna," Sam finishes the story. "And she was no Backwoods Barbie. That implies she might be hot. Keri Lynn Casey was woof, woof."

"Shut up bro," Travis yells. He's shaking. I don't blame him—

"It's been a long afternoon. How about we go home and have some sweet tea on the porch," I suggest. I'm sure Travis wants to hide somewhere for a while and go over in his head another thousand times what he did to deserve the break-up and fake-baby from Keri Lynn Casey. Well, not fake-baby. I suppose she has someone's baby out in Louisiana, it's just not Travis's baby.

The boat engine roars back to life and we cruise through the swamp marshes with wind in our hair, watching the black glimmer of gator eyes dunk down under the water as we fly by.

Home. I said, *how about we go home*.

And I'm actually starting to feel it... the connection to this place, these people. Their lives. Their stories.

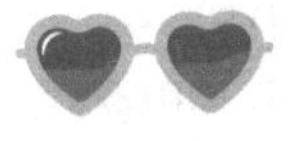

14

RUSTED FORD TRUCK

I'M IN THE BATHROOM getting ready for another day of riding around in the swamp or going to the barn. Or maybe today we will start in the garage and work on the cars before the sweltering summer sun beats down on the tin roof, making it unbearable. I learned pretty quickly that wearing all my make-up and perfume is not necessary out here. I'm not trying to impress my cousins and all it does is attract the bugs anyway. So getting ready goes a lot faster.

The door to my room opens and closes.

"Hello?" I ask and peek out of the bathroom. My mom comes bouncing in like she has every right to be here with me.

"Rian, how about we spend some time together to-day?" She asks. My eyes roll hard. I've hardly seen her, except at meals. Everyone who works at Cullier Manor House has a seat at the dinner table. Which means there's like twenty people and lots of talking and laughing. I've been sitting as far away from Mom as possible and sneaking out after dinner before she can corner me.

I'm still mad at her.

I know I should be over it!

But, for some reason, clinging to my anger is the only thing I have with Mom. If I let her off the hook, I'll be admitting that maybe she was right. Maybe I needed a change. Maybe I was ready to shed the whole New York Princess thing.

"No, I have plans," I tell her. I'm pulling my hair back into a bun, it feels nice off my neck, and keeps the back of me cool in my gray spaghetti strapped tank top paired with a pair of holey jean shorts. I'm calling my new style, *country sheik.*

"Your hair looks lovely, pulled up, like that" she says and reaches to touch, but I jerk my head away from her.

"Travis drives the ATV like an animal. My hair gets in my eyes if I don't pull it back," I tell her.

"Rian, have I done something? You've hardly spoken to me since we got here. I thought maybe we'd have some time together, you know, before Darcy gets back from New York." She seems sad. I'm annoyed. I grab my mascara and start putting it on. I know I'll regret it later when I get splashed on the boat or no-see-ums get stuck in my lashes. That's what Travis calls the little invisible bugs that you can feel crawling on your face, but you can't see them.

"Well, you moved me away from my home. You brought me to a place that I didn't even know existed. And you've gone from uptight New York divorce lawyer to a country Queen! You're what? Taking over the fishing lure business that gramps started and Aunt Kris turned into some empire. I'm not really sure, since you lied to me my entire life. I mean, do you even know what the hell you're doing?" I turn to look at her. She looks tired.

"Rian."

"You look like shit Mom." I push past her and walk out of the room. I know that last comment cut her. Her image has always been so important to her. But, then she just let it fall away when we left New York. She wanted this life here right? To swoop in and rescue my cousins and this house and this place. But, it seems to me it was doing just fine before we showed up.

Except of course for Uncle Chuck murdering Aunt Kris.

Which, by the way, why doesn't anyone want to talk about what happened? It's almost like the entire murder-suicide never happened at all...

"No. You just stop right there," Mom is shouting at me as I'm running down the stairs, past all the old southern belles. "Rian, STOP!"

"I have places to go and people to see," I shout one of Mom's famous lines over my shoulder and keep running until I reach the kitchen.

"Miss Rian, there you are! Whoa, slow down," Mrs. Day scolds when I come charging through the doors at full speed, nearly taking out the cook Mrs. Paula. "Sam said he wanted the big basket. The boys have something special planned for you today." Mrs. Day hands me a huge wooden basket. What on earth would Sam want this for?

"Uh, okay." I take the basket from her and grab a banana from the bowl on the counter. I was kind of hoping to stay for biscuits or some smothered grits. I'm actually kind of loving the food here. But, I'd never tell Ava or anyone else back home.

"Yuck, you're so gross. Grits?" I can almost hear Ava now.

"Out you go, the boys are waiting," Mrs. Day shoos me out of the side door that leads to the sun porch just as Mom is coming into the kitchen.

"Rian, wait," Mom puts her hand up, but I run out, feeling an awful lot like little red riding hood running away from the wolf in grandma's clothing.

When I reach the front of the house, Sam is standing there, leaning oh-so-casually against the stone stairs, with a stupid grin on his face.

"Why do you look like that?" I hold out the basket that Mrs. Day sent with me.

"Cause me and Travis have a real treat for you Rian. A city girl like you ain't never seen nothin like this." He takes the basket and then starts running.

"Wait for me!" I yell and chase after him. But dang, Sam is fast.

"Come on Rian! Hurry up!" He shouts. On the edge of the driveway, where the gravel part meets the asphalt is an old Ford pick-up truck. One I've not seen yet during our exploration on the property. It's rusted red and covered in mud. Sam jumps over the tailgate and into the back with one quick movement. Travis is in the driver's seat and makes a crowing sound and blasts the horn. It startles me. He's wearing his tattered tan cowboy hat, which only means one thing– they are totally up to something crazy.

"What in the hell are you two up to?" I slow down. The truck is so loud. There's music blasting and I swear it is way too early in the day for this. But, what do I know about country boys? After this week with Sam and Travis, I've realized they do things their own way, that's for sure.

"Get in!" Sam reaches over the tail of the truck bed and helps pull me up into the back. I awkwardly climb in. "Betcha never did that in New York!" He shouts as Travis guns it the moment I sit down. I scream as we go flying down the driveway. I hold on for dear life and Sam is all grins. His blond hair whipping in the wind.

"Where are we going?" I yell. Robert must have heard us coming, because when I look around the next corner, I see he has the gate open and he's waving at us as Travis speeds through.

"Don't worry about it," he says.

"Oh sure, that's easy for you to say!"

"Eat your banana and enjoy the ride," Sam points. I look down. I forgot I still had it in my hand. I've squished it. Gross. Instead of eating it, I throw it over my shoulder and it hits the road where it will blister until some hungry animal comes along and licks it up.

My stomach protests.

Sam is singing along to the music, his voice loud and twangy, full of life, while Travis continues to drive around like a maniac. We are on back roads and sometimes he cuts through a grass field then through high spots in swampy marshes. I have no idea where we are going. I smile thinking about how the NYP's would react if I told them I was riding in the back of an old red truck listening to country music and driving in the swamp.

The truck slows down as we approach a huge bridge over a salt marsh. There are wild orange trees on either side. It's like something from a vintage postcard saying, Welcome to Florida.

15

POND APPLES

FINALLY, TRAVIS PULLS UP to an old house and turns off his truck. Hardly a house. More like a shack. The wide wooden planks that make up the siding are falling off. The tin roof is rusted and tender green shoots from swamp weeds are growing out of the janky gutters. A hot gust of wind whips by, smelling like rotted muck and oranges.

"What is this place?" I ask, cautiously looking around. It's like something from a horror movie– this is where the car breaks down and someone with a chainsaw is out back hacking up bloody bodies. The hair on my neck stands up.

"This is the old settler's cabin," Sam says as he jumps out of the truck and opens the tail gate so I can crawl down. I've never been more thankful to have my feet on solid ground.

"And what, exactly, are *we* doing here?" I ask. Then I remember all their begging and pleading to take me on some hunt for pirate treasure and Native American ruins. If they tricked me into a mud quest, I'm going to have some words with them.

"Come on, it's behind the cabin." Travis walks up and puts his hand on my shoulder. I jump a foot. "Why so jumpy, cous?"

"Uh, what's behind the cabin Travis?" I take a few steps back towards the truck. A crow caws and flaps from a tree near us, sending leaves raining on my head. I scream and crouch down, throwing my hands over my head for protection.

"I don't want to die." I start hyperventilating as intrusive thoughts race through my mind. The wind licks my face again and I swear I hear a woman scream in the distance.

Sam laughs. "Rian." He crouches down next to me and pats my back. "It was just a bird. Don't go all New York priss on us now– Come on! Let's go pick apples."

"Apples?" I look over my shoulder.

Sam stands and extends a hand to me. I clasp his strong fingers and stand up, gently brushing myself off.

"Not just any apples," Sam says. The sun shines brightly across the bridge of his nose and he has a big grin on his face. I know for damn sure there's a scowl still spread across mine.

"Oh yeah, are there other kinds of apples?" My hands rest on my hips. All this for some stupid apples?

"Pond apples!" Sam and Travis shout at the same time.

Okay, so I'm not about to die. I'm about to pick fruit. My skin tightens and my lips purse. I want to say something cruel, like who the hell do you think I am? But Sam picks up the basket and runs at full speed around the house. Travis is hot on his heels.

"Ugh. Wait!" But they don't stop. "Hello! Wait for me!" I shout and I chase after them. A burst of energy surges through my legs and I run at full speed, completely forgetting that I was scared only moments ago.

When I turn the corner, around the edge of the Old Settlers Cabin, I finally see what all the fuss was about. As far as the eye can see are rows of old trees with twisted, knobby branches, heavy with leaves and covered in green speckled fruit. Apples. My breath hitches in my throat. It's like nothing I've ever seen in my life.

I'm frozen, gazing out at the old orchard.

It's not been groomed, or trimmed, or taken care of in a very long time... It's wild, just like everything else in the Everglades.

"Watch out for gators, Rian!" Sam laughs as he runs and jumps and grabs a pond apple off the closest tree. He looks like he does when we play basketball in the barn, but except for rushing for a layup, he's rushing the tree and leaping up to pluck down the fruit. I'm slack-jawed.

"You okay?" Travis trots back over to where I'm standing and drops his cowboy hat. Then he plops in a handful of the strange new fruit into it.

"I, uh," the words escape me. "I've never seen anything like this." I just stand and stare at the wondrous, expansive orchard.

"Pretty sweet, huh?" Travis runs back out to collect more fruit.

My feet are planted like roots, and I watch as my cousins run and jump and hop from tree to tree and grab the fruit like they've done this a thousand times before. They throw the apples and they land in the basket or near the basket. After a few minutes, I snap to my senses and rush over and pick up the fruit that misses the basket, and put them in.

"Can I ask, what are we going to do with all these?"

"Cobbler of course." Sam pauses his fruit pursuit and puts his hand up to block the sun. "Justine makes the best cobbler outta pond apples." Sam smiles.

"Justine?" I ask.

"Yeah, you've met her right?" Sam asks.

"I've seen her around a few times. She offered to take me shopping." I fold my arms over my chest remembering how annoying that first time I met her was. But, even so, I can't help the heat from rising up in my face as I think about our encounter in the kitchen yesterday. The way she smiled and told me I looked good in my red and white striped bikini.

"Wow, I'm surprised Justine offered to take you shopping. She's usually a complete sour-puss," Sam says.

"Yeah, I can see that," I reply. I did get a bitchy vibe from her.

"She used to live with us when her folks died. Mama sort of adopted her. Big Jackie isn't really the *raising a little girl on his own* kind of big brother. He's great for fixing cars and managing the property, but could you picture him playing dolls or brushing hair?" Sam climbs up another tree and starts tossing down more pond apples.

"His hands are so big he probably couldn't hold a brush." I laugh. "So, where does Justine live now?" I ask.

"She still lives with us. But in one of the smaller houses, the one with the pink flowers growing on the side, close to Travis's shop. She's super smart and graduated highschool a few years ago when she was sixteen. Mama offered to pay for her to go to college anywhere she wanted, but Justine said college was for stuck-up assholes." Sam rolls his eyes. But I don't disagree. College is for stuck-up assholes.

"So what does she do now?"

"Well, Mama said if she wasn't going to college, she had to work and earn her way. Said it will be the same for me and Travis if we don't go to college. I wonder if Aunt Tori will stick to that?" Sam looks at me, like I'm supposed to know if my Mom will make him go to college or get a job.

"Well, maybe I will take Justine up on her offer to go shopping one of these days," I say after thinking about it for a while. I wouldn't mind going to pick up a few things for riding around in the side-by-side. I already ruined three sundresses this week that cost more than Travis's truck. I guess, if it's for getting clothes for going mudding, I can stomach going discount shopping. Oh God! Just the thought of polyester makes my skin crawl. But, on the other hand I would get some alone time with Justine.

Which could be flirty and interesting.

I hope my cousins don't see the heat rising in my face.

"CATCH!" Travis is racing back towards us and throws one of the apples at me. I scream and duck and that sets Sam into complete hysterics.

"Jerk!" I pick an apple off the ground and throw it at Travis. He catches it easily.

"You throw like a girl." He smirks. I try throwing another one, even harder this time. He catches it with no problem and lobs it into the basket.

"When you said I was in for a real treat, this wasn't what I expected," I say to Sam.

"Oh cous, but they are a treat. Try one," he urges me. I make a face.

"Come on scaredy cat," he picks one off a tree and tosses it to me. I give it a once over. I mean, I guess it looks okay, no worm holes or black spots. I take a bite and it's sweet and tangy and tastes like the orange melon balls they serve at the country club in the Hamptons.

"Mmmmm," I reply and take another bite. Travis puts a few more into the basket which is practically overflowing. "Does anyone else come and pick these? There are so many!" I say and point to all the apples that are on the ground.

"Gators eat em. Their other name is Gator Apples. See look." Travis points to a patch of taller grass, maybe ten feet away, that looks a lot swampier than the tuft we are standing on. I see a pair of eyes attached to a dark green leather snout. It stands out against the light, sun-blistered grass and the sun reflects off its eyes. I automatically take two steps backwards and run into Sam.

"Whoa, remember what I taught you. The little baby gators can't hurt you," Sam reminds me. He's been giving me lessons when we are out on the boat, teaching me all about the various creatures in the swamp.

"Well, you said baby gators mean mama gators can be close by. I don't want to be near a mama when she's done eating apples and wants fresh meat. Since the basket's full, can we go home now?" I ask.

"You know Rian, out about a mile, past the pond apples, that's where the pirate ship is," Travis says. He sounds so serious I almost believe him.

"Oh yeah." I roll my eyes.

"That's why the old timers settled here. They thought they'd find Black Beard's treasure buried in the swamp. But, no one ever found the treasure, far as we can tell, just the ship." Travis wiggles his blonde eyebrows. But I'm still not buying what he's trying to sell.

"Pirate ships and buried treasure." I wipe the sweat off the back of my neck and rub my palms on the fabric of my tank top. "How long are you gonna keep it up?"

Sam bats away a curious bee. "Yep, real Spanish gold and jewels. They say it was buried 'round here, after his ship got blown in during a Hurricane. Mama loved the history of this place, she has all kinds of old documents in the library." But there's a twinkle in his eye.

"You're such liars!" I laugh.

"Scouts honor," Sam holds up his hand and tries to keep a straight face.

"Oh shut up Sam, you're hardly a boy scout," I tease back.

"Suit yourself. Me and Travis will just come out treasure hunting on our own." Sam uses the fear of missing out to tempt me.

I shake my head no.

"How 'bout we go home and get some grub. I'm starved!" Sam bumps his shoulder against mine. I don't have to be told twice. The sun is high in the sky and my stomach is turning in knots. A few bites of some swamp fruit is not enough for me.

After Travis and Sam load the basket of pond apples and I crawl into the truck bed, Travis yells, "HOLD ON!" The truck jerks forward and I barely have time to put my arms out to brace myself against the hot metal as he zooms down the dirt roads, sliding from side to side. We fly through the swampy air, weaving through the oak trees and pastures and between the ratty palms. And like before, Robert has the gate open for us and we cruise through it without a care in the world. He waves and winks at me, like he knew it wouldn't take long for this place to make a home under my skin.

This place is your legacy.

God I hate when Mom is right.

Travis slows down and turns off the music when we pull up to the house. He jumps out and takes off in a sprint toward his shop. He has more energy than anyone I ever met. Sam's nice enough to let the back down so I can jump down before he heaves the basket of pond apples down to the ground. "You want me to take these inside?" He asks, glancing over his shoulder at Travis.

"I got it," I say. I don't know why I said that. I am not strong at all.

"Alright cous, we'll be out in the shop, come find us later." Sam jumps in the driver's side and the truck roars to life. He drives on the gravel and out towards the shop.

I manage to lug the heavy basket onto the front porch before I go inside.

"MRS. PAULA!" I scream.

The cook comes rushing out frantically. "Lord help me, is everything okay?" She has flour on her face and in her hair.

"Yeah, why wouldn't it be?" I ask. "There's a basket of pond apples on the porch for you to cook with, can you make someone bring them inside?" Then I go running up the stairs, leaving Mrs. Paula with a simmering gaze in her eyes.

16

SECRETS & SECRET DOORS

I SHOULD HAVE KNOWN a house this big would hold secrets. I mean, I know my mom has secrets. Every day she's out running this mysterious fishing lure company that I know nothing about. And my cousins do too... I don't spend every waking minute with them. There are plenty of times they are off doing god knows what, and I have no idea where they are. See, there's a lingering feeling, heavy like the local humidity, everywhere, things are more than what they first appear. The truth is, I care, I really do. But is it enough to get in the middle of it and ask questions?

I'm more of a let it fester under the surface kind of girl.

Until I can't stand it any longer—then I'll squeeze it to a big, pussy head.

Yeah, total vomit. I agree.

"What do you mean there's secrets?" Ava asks. I have her on speaker phone while I'm in my clawfoot tub, soaking and shaving my legs. I hear a familiar noise in the background, she's walking outside and taxis are honking. My heart clenches. Fuck I miss that! Walking around the streets of the city. It's also super annoying, because she's not paying attention to me.

"I said, secret passageways, aren't you even listening to me?" I pull the razor over my leg, making sure to go slow around my knee cap and up my thigh.

"Sorry, my driver dropped me a full block away from the restaurant," she says. I hear someone shouting and she yells, "Yeah fuck you too buddy!"

I giggle. How can I be annoyed with her?

"Sorry. Tell me about the passageway," she says.

So for the next ten minutes, while I finish bathing, I tell her all about the various passageways Sam has shown me in the house. There's one in the kitchen pantry and one in the library and one that goes from the upstairs all the way down to the laundry room. But that's more of a laundry shoot, I guess.

"Wait, it's like the Algonquin Hotel, you know they have dumbwaiters in the Penthouse suite," she exclaims.

"Oh my god, you're right! Remember when we stayed there and dropped apples down it?" My cheeks hurt from smiling so big as I climb out of the tub.

"Your dad was so pissed. Didn't we get his membership banned?" She asks through a breathy laugh. "Oh shit, Maggie and Gina are here. I gotta go, Rian. Love ya!" The phone goes silent before I can even say goodbye.

I can't help it, but my lip curls into a hideous snarl, and I drop my head and clench my fists. Ugh. My friends are all about to have some amazing Saturday brunch followed by a day on the town, and I'm stuck here, doing the same thing with my cousins. Sure, it's been fun the last few weeks, but god, what I wouldn't give for a day with my girls.

"Rian!" A familiar voice rings outside my door, snapping me out of my funk. "I'm back!"

It's Darcy!

"Be right there, just getting dressed." I call out and run to my closet. I grab my pastel pink Sister Jane dress with a wide white collar and shimmy it on over my head. Then I pull the clips from my hair and let it swoop down over my shoulders. I shake it out a few times before I head out to see mom's assistant.

She's lingering on the landing of the stairs, like she isn't sure if she's coming or going. I don't hide the smirk on my face. "Hey Darcy, I didn't know you were coming back today."

Her eyes bulge from her head. "I can't believe how tan you've gotten in a couple of weeks! Gosh Rian, you look great." Darcy gushes.

I look her up and down. She looks different too. She's not wearing that severe NY business ponytail and her dark hair is long and wavy. She's ditched her usual black turtleneck for a bright blue wrap dress and a pair of, oh my god.

"Are you wearing Birkenstocks? Seriously?" I mean, what is she thinking? That is so gross.

"You caught me! These are my Vermont summer shoes. I thought maybe I could pull them off here." She smiles sweetly with an 'oh well' kind of shrug then turns to head down the stairs.

"No. Wait, please," I beg. She stops and looks at me. "You can't wear those shoes, not here, not ever." I shake my head furiously. We might be in the middle of BFE Florida, but please, I cannot let this kind of fashion travesty happen, not on my watch. "Don't you have any slides or something leathery with a strap. Anything that doesn't scream granola eating Subaru driver."

Her cheeks flush crimson, like the sunset on the edge of the swamp, and she puts her hand up to stop me as I open my mouth to keep going. "Okay, okay, Rian, I get it, you can stop anytime now."

"Are you sure? Because if I was you, I wouldn't keep walking down the stairs, I'd be going back to my room to change." I point to her room. Partly because she must be scared my Mom will think the same thing, or partly because she's placating me, Darcy does go back to her room and change her shoes.

She comes out, her face back to its normal color.

I look down at her feet and gasp. "Toe ring leathers? Seriously Darcy." She's wearing another pair of equally nauseating shoes.

"God, Rian. In the city I wear heels, every day, even in the summer. When you work at a law firm you wear black heels. Period. And on the weekend, well, I wear Birkenstocks." She's pouting and folds her arms over her chest. I've obviously gotten under her skin.

"What size are you? I'm going shopping with Justine. I'll get you something appropriate." I put my hands on my hips and wait. She stares at me for a minute, I can tell she's thinking it over in her head.

"Fine. I'm a ten."

I laugh. "No wonder you don't have any good shoes, or a boyfriend. You have HUGE feet!"

She huffs and marches down the stairs, tired of me picking on her. I laugh and run back to my room and slam the door shut and lean against it with a wicked smile across my face. I don't know why I just did Darcy dirty like that. For fun I guess. Or because it's how I always was back home, and I know Darcy from back home in New York.

I let out a long sigh. A feeling like shame creeps up my limbs and makes my ears tingle. A brush it off.

"I guess next time I see Justine, I'll tell her I want to go shopping after all," I say loudly to whatever ghosts are listening.

I spend the next few hours, sitting at my desk, hunched over a pad of paper with a piece of charcoal wedged between my thumb and pointer finger, sketching pictures. People I've seen around the property. The boat and the swamp. I even sketch one of the little baby gator eyes, all black and glassy. I'm lost in the moment, happy to stay here forever, until my stomach starts growling. I lean back, my neck and shoulders tight, and sniff the air. Something smells heavenly, wafting up from the kitchen. So I drop the charcoal and drag myself off the chair and follow my nose down to investigate. But, right as I'm about to push open the door to the kitchen, and devour whatever is making that yummy smell, I hear people arguing in hushed voices behind the swinging door.

I drop my arms and lean my head closer, hoping I can hear through the wood.

"You can't tell her," says one of the voices.

"The hell I can't. Watch me," says a second person.

"You bitch," says the first voice.

I slap a hand over my mouth and look around. This is some drama! Where is Sam when I need him? Whoever is on the other side of this door is heated, they even dropped the b-word. Which, from what I've learned, is not the kind of language they use around this place. No one here curses at all. It's all *golly-gee* and *ah-shucks* and bullshit like that.

The voices are talking again, but they've moved away from the door and I can't make out a thing they are saying. I need to get closer, without them seeing me.

And I know just the place!

I sneak through the front parlor room, past the grand piano and fireplace then I race down the hall that goes behind the huge grand formal dining room. On the other side of that is a butler's pantry where they keep all the antique dishes. Once I get into the tight space where the crystal goblets are stored, I look around to make sure know one has seen me, then I use the secret sliding door Sam showed me a few days ago when Mrs. Day and Mrs. Paula were having a screaming match about the amount of shrimp you're supposed to add to something called Shrimp Clemenceau.

Just like today, I was about to walk into the kitchen, when I heard shouting. But this time, Sam was behind me and snatched my arm, pulling me back to safety. "Don't go in there unless you want your head bitten off," he hissed.

"But I'm starved!" I complained.

"Follow me. There's an easier way to get food without being seen." And I followed him through the house until we were inside of the pantry.

It's an impressive room, filled floor to ceiling with shelves of glass mason jars canned with everything you can imagine. Sliced peaches, bright red jams, green leafy stuff, creamy looking soups, and all kinds of rice and pasta. There are shelves filled with bags of flour and sugar and tubs of lard (bleh!). But Sam said that's what you make pie crust from. So I have to remember not to eat pie here. On one of the shelves, Sam showed me where the regular food is. There's stuff that's easy to grab and go, like cereal bars and mini muffins.

But now, stomach-be-damned! I'm not here for food, even if that was the reason I went toward the kitchen in the first place.

I'm here to eavesdrop.

Like I said, this place is full of secrets.

I put my ear against the door, the one that leads into the kitchen. But, the voices are still too muffled for me to hear. I carefully crack the pantry door just a teensy bit. Honestly, I don't know why I care. I mean, whatever dumb crap these people have to argue about is none of my concern. But, maybe it's because I haven't had any other drama to entertain me this week. Okay, all that stuff on the boat about Keri Lynn Casey and Travis was pretty juicy. But, this is real live action. I'd grown so used to fighting back home between Mom and Dad, I actually sort of miss it in a twisted way.

"Justine, listen to me. If you go blabbing your fat mouth we might all be in for it, seeing as how none of us stopped what was goin on. You really want to lose your job and your house?"

"Get off me, Annona," Justine hisses.

Annona? Who the hell is Annona? I wedge my body forward and move around a sack of flour, to get a better view through the crack of the pantry door, but I can't see a damn thing. Wait, Justine is moving. Her arms flap up and down. "I don't need your permission to tell her what really happened. I'm the one who has to live with it. Not you!"

I don't know what is going on, but maybe I should intervene? My heart pounds.

"FINE then, go, tell Miss Tori. See if I care!"

"Maybe I fucking will and don't get me started about nobody stopping what was going on here. You of all people should know better than that." Justine spits out the last part.

Seriously, what the hell is going on?

Justine has a secret she's keeping from my Mom. I knew there was something fishy about this place, well besides the fishing lures.

I take a step backwards when I hear the back door slam shut. It's followed by some banging on pots and pans. I don't want to get caught so I tip-toe back the way I came and stealthily make my way out of the house, through the front door, taking each step as even and regular as a can until I reach the fountain. I don't want to look suspicious, but as soon as I reach the spurting water and hear the birds chirping, I take off in a sprint.

I need to find Sam and Travis, ASAP!

Something is brewing and I'm going to find out what.

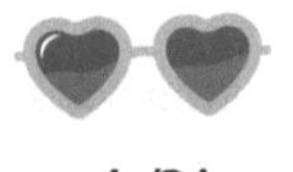

17

TEENAGE SLEUTH

I TEXT SAM 9-1-1 as I run towards the shop. The white collar on my dress is choking me and the expensive fabric has hardly any give. Every movement is constricting. When I get close enough I think someone will hear, I start shouting. "SAM! Where are you? SAM!"

No answer.

"TRAVIS!" I yell. The gravel crunches under my feet and the sun reflects against the tin, amplifying the heat rising in my face. But the shop is quiet and I'm out of breath from my run and yelling. I look around in a panic. It's so hot, they are probably out on the skiff fishing. I glance toward the overgrown trees on the other side of the shop, and a shiver runs up my spine. I really don't want to walk the trail all the way to the dock by myself. What if I run into a python, or something worse?

I'm pretty sure I can manage to drive one of the side-by-sides... Big Jackie keeps the keys labeled in a box on the wall. So without giving it another thought, I run to the out-building that has the ATV's and snag the pair of keys before I can talk myself out of it. I get into one and I'm just about to start it up when my phone buzzes.

Oh thank god!

It's Sam. He wants to know if 9-1-1 means a real emergency or just some girl crap.

"God, dummy," I say out loud and check the review mirror, and jump when I see the reflection of a person, walking between the buildings. It's Justine. She looks pissed.

I have two options. I can drive out of here and find Sam and Travis, to ask if they know who Annona is and why Justine was arguing with her. Or, I could grow a pair and ask Justine myself. Maybe I'm stupid. But I leave the keys in the ignition and climb out of the vehicle and run towards her. Option two it is.

"Hey Justine, wait up!" I shout and wave my arms so she can see me.

"Rian." She acknowledges me, but she's not slowing down, clearly on a mission to get anywhere but here.

I know that feeling. I've battled it myself recently.

"Wait, slow down." I grab for her elbow, my fingers brush gently across her skin, but she's moving too fast for it to have any effect. "Are you okay?" I ask.

"Why wouldn't I be okay Rian?" She turns around. She's wearing a pair of cut off jean shorts and a flowy yellow tank. Her hair is pinned over to one side and smoothed in finger waves. Like an old picture of Bette Davis. Even with her lips pouting and eyes dark from anger, she looks– beautiful. Should I tell her? Maybe it would make her feel better.

"I heard you and Annona arguing," I admit.

She shakes her head and turns to keep walking. I'm like a lost puppy dog, I follow her, step for step, until we reach the porch of her little house. The one with the pretty pink flowers growing up the side of it.

I look at her.

She looks at me.

A stand-off... She doesn't budge as she folds her arms over her chest and it feels like we stare at one another forever. Finally, I give in.

"If you aren't going to tell me what's wrong, that's okay. I have something else I want to talk to you about. Would you take me shopping tomorrow? I need to buy shoes for Darcy. She has stupid shoes."

Her posture changes, and she lets her arms fall to her side. The breath she was holding in our stare down, hisses gently from her lips, and her mouth curls into a smile. Her eyes brighten.

"Yeah, we can go shoe shopping." She nods and turns to grab the handle to the screen door, but pauses and looks back at me, staring deep into my eyes. "Oh, whatever you think you heard in the kitchen, is none of your business." Then she goes inside and slams the door in my face.

I laugh. Did she really think she could just slam the door and this conversation would be over?

Knock, knock.

"What? I said I'd take you," Justine says when she opens her door and sees me standing there.

"Yeah, well, maybe you should have some of that southern hospitality I hear everyone yapping about and invite me into your house," I tell her. I put my hands on my hips so she knows I mean business. She looks me up and down and I think maybe she's going to slam the door on me again. But, instead she grins.

"You aren't going to leave, are you?"

"Nope."

She sighs, then opens the screen door and lets me inside. I don't know what to expect when I go inside of an eighteen year old's house. But it's not this. The walls are painted black with gold geometric shapes hand-painted to look like vintage wallpaper. There are several large framed pictures of 1930's art deco prints in bright reds and yellows. In the center of the room is a navy blue couch with gold buttons tufting the fabric in a diamond pattern. It all takes my breath away, it's so my vibe, it hurts.

"You want some sweet tea?" Justine asks, and before I can say yes or no, she heads into the kitchen leaving me to make myself at home. It's the size of an average New York City apartment. Of course, I grew up in a penthouse on the top floor of my building, so I don't really know. But, I mean, I think this is what most people live like in New York.

Small spaces.

I keep looking around. Justine has tons of house plants, their green leaves and vines winding around the room. And on the farthest wall, there are so many pictures of her and Sam and Travis and Aunt Kris and Big Jackie. I guess Sam wasn't joking when he said Aunt Kris had adopted her. I don't see any pictures of a boyfriend or girlfriend or other friends and family. But, that's not why I'm here. *I'm not here to spy on Justine.*

Of course it's a bonus to see inside her life.

She's busy getting ice from the vintage mint green fridge in her galley style kitchen, which is really just part of the living space, so I can watch everything she's doing. She carefully puts the ice in tall skinny glasses with opaque rose and geometric shapes etched into the sides of them.

"Do you like vintage?" I ask.

"What was your first clue?" She hands me one of the glasses then plops down on her sofa. I follow her lead and plop down too. Then we both sip on the super sugary sweet tea. I'm not sure I'll ever get used to it. But, it's all they serve and it's cold and that's what counts when you are in the swamp. Come to think of it, it's awfully hot in here.

"God, don't you have air conditioning?" I whine.

"Awe, is the poor little Rian hot?" she teases and gets up to turn down the thermostat. It kicks in right away and the icy cold air blasts down from a vent in the ceiling. The beads of sweat evaporate from my face, and I sigh with relief.

"Thank you." I say a little on the snotty side. But, I think Justine can handle it.

"Alright, so, I invited you in for tea. You've experienced southern hospitality," she says when she sits back down. This time she kicks her feet up on her wooden coffee table. Her toes are painted a soft pale pink. It looks nice. So do her legs, they are smooth and I want to reach out and feel them. But, that might be crossing a line. Plus, I'm not here to flirt. I'm here to find out what that fight was over. I need answers.

"Thank you," I say more politely this time.

She laughs.

"Are you going to tell me what happened? Or do I have to beg?"

"I don't know what you mean?" She smirks.

I sit up tall. "I heard you! You and someone named Annona were fighting. You called her a bitch and she said not to tell my Mom something because she wouldn't understand why none of you stopped something from happening." I pause for dramatic effect. "Justine, I want to know what that was all about." I place my empty glass on the table next to her feet. "Actually, I deserve to know what that was all about."

Her glass is empty now too, the chunky ice cubes are jingling as she twirls it around. She looks at me. Her eyes, slowly assessing. Probably deciding how much to tell me or maybe she's going to tell me to fuck off and it will be her word against mine if I go and tell my Mom on her for cursing me out.

"I was going to tell your Mama where your Aunt and Uncle hid the treasure. I'm the only one who knows and Annona thinks I should keep my mouth shut, that your Mama doesn't deserve to have it, since she already has all the fishing lure money," Justine says, pretty matter of fact. I look at her. Then I just watch her swirl and shake the ice in her glass again. "Well, anything else Nancy Drew?"

"Nancy Drew? Does it look like I'm a red-headed nerd trying to solve a mystery? And hidden treasure? Do you think I'm an idiot?" First Sam and Travis, now Justine, with this stupid treasure myth. My mouth hangs open, because I want to say more, but I can't decide if I should just scream instead.

She takes one look at me and bursts out laughing.

And I want to stay mad, I do, but she looks so cute laughing. And when I think about it, it is sort of funny, and I start laughing with her.

"I'm gonna call you Nancy from now on." She gets up and takes our glasses back to the kitchen and pours more sweet tea.

"If you're going to call me Nancy, then–" I stand up and walk towards her to get the tea.

"Then what?" She faces me. We are inches apart.

The color rises in my cheeks, hot and tingly. Um... I'm not sure why I got this close to her. All I really wanted to do was find out what her and Annona were fighting about. But, it's nice to be with her, to joke and tease and be around a girl again. Spending all this time with Travis and Sam, and hardly talking to Ava or Gina or Maggie for weeks, I didn't realize I needed this.

"Then I'm going to call you–" But, I don't know what to say and my throat starts going dry even though I've been drinking all this sweet tea. Justine inches closer to me.

"Say it," she whispers.

Oh my god. We are in uncharted waters here. Are we flirting? Are we having a moment? Are we going to kiss? A second passes, but it feels like an eternity. Her pupils dilate and she blinks once.

"Say it. What are you going to call me, Nancy?" She bites her bottom lip, ever so slowly and I go completely weak in the knees. The drum of my heartbeat pounds in my ears and I see a muscle tick in Justine's neck.

And then for some unknown, pathetic, dopy reason I say, in about my least sexiest voice, "Pirate."

Pirate? Really?

I smack my hand against my forehead and we both burst into laughter.

"You're stupid. You've been hanging with Travis and Sam too much. Pirate? That's the best you could come up with?" Justine laughs again.

I'm mortified because I should have said something else. Something cute, something clever, something tempting... but I went with pirate? Thankfully, my phone starts blowing up, easing the awkwardness growing between us. We walk back over to the couch and sit down.

I check the screen, it's Sam. He's freaking out because they came back to find me and I'm not in the Big House or anywhere else they have looked. Oh yeah, I guess I should have told him the 9-1-1 was off.

"Seriously, what were you fighting about? Because I know it wasn't about treasure. That's ridiculous."

"Now, why is that so ridiculous? I know you were out there the other day. I saw the basket of pond apples. I'm sure Sam took you out to the pirate ship," she says and folds her arms.

"Uh, yeah we went to get the apples. But, I didn't see a pirate ship. I mean Jesus. You all must think I'm a dumb-ass! Pirate Treasure? Hushed fights. I mean, I'm having a hard enough time dealing with this entire fishing lure empire shit. Don't get me started on buried treasure."

"Rian!"

"RIAN!"

My cousin's voices are loud and close.

"I'M IN HERE!" I scream back.

"God, go outside if you want to scream. Anyway, believe what you want. I'll take you shopping tomorrow like I said. But we have to go early, be here at nine. Now get out of my house." Justine gets up and walks over to the door and opens it for me. The boys are both walking in as she's trying to walk me out.

"Good, take her, she's annoying," Justine tells them.

"Rude!" I say and walk out with Sam and Travis right behind me. I'm fuming, steam is literally pouring out of my ears. Justine is such a little liar! I mean, fine, she didn't want to tell me why she and mysterious Annona were arguing. But, she didn't have to lie to my face. And what was that in there anyway? Our faces were an inch apart. So close I could see every perfect pore, every sun soaked freckle, I could have kissed her if I wanted to.

If that was me and Ava, I'd have told her to quit being such a bitch, tell me the truth and then pretend to be annoyed when she snuggled up to me in bed. But, I don't see me and Justine having a sleepover anytime soon. My face feels flushed again with the thought of being in a bed with Justine.

As soon as we are out of earshot, I throw my hands up in the air. "Justine is so annoying. I mean, what was all that crap about!"

Sam trots up next to me as I'm stomping away and puts his arm around me. "What the heck is goin on cous? You texted 9-1-1, ain't that like serious trouble?"

"What's going on? Well, first, everyone here is keeping secrets," my voice raises an octave and I shove Sam's arm off me.

"Secrets?" Travis says with a nervous edge and pushes his hair back.

I glare at him. "Oh what, do you have a secret you'd like to share?" Then, that annoying bell rings from the Big House, loud enough we can all hear it.

"Saved by the bell. Mint Julep, yes please!" he laughs and goes galloping off, completely ignoring me.

"Oh really. Like my Mom's going to let him drink with her. He's so stupid!" I don't tell Sam that Mom used to let me have wine with her back home. Instead I just head the same way Travis ran off to. Maybe I can help myself to a drink too, if Mom and Darcy are busy blabbing and not paying any attention to me.

"Wait, why don't you slow down and tell me what happened? From the beginning," Sam asks. His voice is genuine and he looks at me with those big puppy dog eyes.

I heave a sigh. "Fine." So I tell him about the kitchen argument and sneaking into the pantry like he showed me and then trying to find him tend Travis and running into Justine and going into her house. Finally, I tell him she said they were arguing about treasure.

He lets out a long and beautiful laugh. I try to stay mad, even though I'm not sure what I'm actually mad about. Maybe because Justine called me Nancy Drew. Like I'm some teenage sleuth trying to solve a mystery. But, that's the last thing I want Justine to think about when she sees me. I want her to see me, like how I was in New York. Confident and perfect. My nails done, my hair done, my nice clothes. I feel so unlike who I used to be, but not who or what I'm supposed to be now. My heart feels like it's beating too fast.

Maybe I'm just tired and hungry.

"One thing you'll learn about Justine is she's got a twisted sense of humor. Her and Mama had that in common. She's just messing with you. But, she wouldn't have let you in her house or offered to take you shopping if she didn't want to get to know you," Sam says, maybe just to calm me down, or maybe because it's true.

I look up and realize we've walked all the way back to the house. He opens the door for me and does a silly bow and holds his arm out, "Ladies first." He grins like the Cheshire cat and I roll my eyes.

"Dork." I elbow him as I walk past him into the house. I'm not sure I'll ever get used to the grandeur of this place. But one thing is for sure, I love the cold, powerful air conditioning. It helps bring my temperature down and I feel more relaxed as I follow Sam through the house and out to the back porch. Mrs. Day and Mrs. Paula are sitting and visiting with Mom and Darcy and Big Jackie. Travis is leaning casually against one of the pillars with a mint julep in his hand and Mom isn't batting an eye. I take his lead and help myself. Oh of course, she shoots me a nasty look, but I give her one right back.

But rather than have a fight with me in front of everyone, she winks and turns back to the conversation with Mrs. Day.

"Annona! You are too funny!" she coos.

So, Mrs. Day is Annona! Well I'll be damned. I take a long drink from my glass and try not to choke. Jesus Christ! This is strong. Yuck. But, I force myself to keep a straight face, from the drink and the revelation that Mrs. Day was the person arguing with Justine. Seriously, how did I not catch it earlier? Her voice, the tone.

The bourbon warms my stomach and I am pulled into my own thoughts, whisked away from this moment. I lean against the wall across from Travis, trying to imitate his casual country boy demeanor. Sam has inserted himself on the couch next to Darcy and Mom. They are all blabbing-on about fishing lures and some kind of blaaaaah...

My mind can't concentrate on that.

In my brain, I go back to the kitchen, still blown away that it was Mrs. Day and Justine arguing over telling Mom something. I run the conversation over and over again in my mind.

I still can't get over Justine claiming it was about a ridiculous pirate treasure. What a jerk. I am going to tell her tomorrow when we go shopping. She has a twisted sense of humor huh? Well, she's in for it when we have thirty miles to drive alone. She's never heard a New Yorker on a rant before! I'll have her begging to spill her guts before we hit the 20-mile mark just to get me to shut up about it. I'm so deep down the rabbit hole of what I'm going to say to her to make her talk that I don't realize everyone else has stopped talking. They are staring at me. I take another long pull from the straw in my drink.

"Earth to Rian!" Darcy waves her hands at me. I blink a few times. And then they all laugh.

"What?" I mumble.

"God Rian! Big Jackie just asked you how you liked picking pond apples with the boys the other day?" Mom chastises me.

I shrug my shoulders. "I dunno."

Sam covers for me and launches into a loud unnecessary speech about how much fun we had and how adorable I was catching fruit and throwing it into the basket.

"I'm going to my room," I announce and set my glass down and walk off the back porch. No one tries to stop me. Which is fine by me.

18

WHO IS MOM, REALLY?

THE NEXT MORNING, I'M up as soon as the sun starts shining through the window, casting little rays of dancing light across my eyelids. I check the time, seven, then I rush into the bathroom. I have to wash and blowdry my hair, get dressed, and do my makeup all before nine. Is it so wrong that I want to look good today? I mean, shopping at some dumb outlet store is tragic at best. No, I want to look good for *Justine.*

Yeah, sure, I was super pissed at her yesterday, with that whole treasure bullshit and not telling me what the real argument with Mrs. Day was all about.

But, there's something about Justine I haven't been able to get off my mind. The pout of her lips, the sun kissed freckles splashed across her face, the care and love she put into decorating her space. I even dreamt about her last night– the corners of my mouth turn up, and my toes curl, as I remember the best part of the dream.

With a final brush, my hair looks amazing. I decide to go pick out the perfect outfit while my face lotion sets. Everyone knows you can't apply makeup to a damp face. I'm wrapped in my fluffy, plush, white bathrobe, like the kind they have at the Ritz Carlton. "Hmm..." I open up my closet and stare at the rows of designer dresses, jumpers, and sweaters. I honestly forgot just how many outfits I have, since I can't wear most of them around here. But today, I'm not going mudding on an ATV or fishing or playing basketball in an old barn.

Today I'm going shopping.

I gnaw on my bottom lip, trying to imagine what I would wear back home for a day on Fifth Ave with Ava? I push aside outfit after outfit. I have to look just the right amount of alluring without coming off too strong. I don't know if I'm the kind of person Justine would even be into.

Maybe my Johanna Ortiz sundress, the white one. I pick up the hanger and hold it up to myself. I've gotten so tan lately, it will actually look good on me. When I bought it Ava told me it washed me out, only because she wanted it and we have a strict no buying the same thing policy. It's in my closet though, so you know who won that argument.

I let my robe fall to the floor and slip the crisp white fabric over my head and look at myself in the full length mirror. The wide straps rest gently on my bronze shoulders and the waist cinches in the middle, showing off my figure. It's cut just low enough to be flirty, not low enough to be skanky. And it's the right length, just above my knee.

If Ava could see me now.

I take the time to do a full face of make-up, just like I used to back in New York. And even though I'm getting tan, I still put on some Bobby Brown bronzer for a cheeky glow. But my favorite part is the mascara. I love it. I put on like thirty coats. It's my favorite accessory and today, I won't get it wet on the fishing boat. Sorry boys.

I'm so busy preening and making sure I look just right in case Justine wants to tell me I look good, that I don't realize I have an audience.

"Rian, it's nice to see you get dressed up," Mom muses from behind me. She's standing in the doorway of the bathroom.

"Jesus, don't you knock," I gasp and spin around to look at her.

"I'm sorry, I–" she pauses.

"What. What do you want?"

"I want this weirdness between us to stop. I want to go back to having some kind of a relationship with you Rian. I've given you the space I thought you might need the last few weeks, to get to know Sam and Travis and everyone here. But, you know, we've got to get back into a groove," she says. I can tell she's practiced this speech. It's like one of her arguments in court. *Judge, if you please, you'll see that my client has been straightforward and open with the court, there is no reason to blah, blah, bullshit...*

"Mom, look. I'm not mad at being here anymore. I'm mad that you lied to me. Because of the way you acted when I was growing up, I thought everyone from your past was a hillbilly swamp person. But, now that I know

Sam and Travis and Justine and Big Jackie, I know they are just regular people." I stop and turn around to look at myself in the bathroom mirror. I look different than I did a few weeks ago when we arrived, not so sharp around the edges, I look brighter, healthier.

I close my eyes for a minute to collect my thoughts, what exactly am I trying to say to Mom? I need to get this right. I need to be brave enough to admit what's been eating me alive ever since she told me about Aunt Kris and Uncle Chuck dying and learning we were moving to Florida.

I put my hands on the counter and take a deep breath before I look at her again. "What I'm trying to say is, I feel like you didn't trust me. You pretended to be someone else for Dad, and that's your deal with him, not mine. But, couldn't you have been open with me? Couldn't you have told me that this life was a part of you? I mean, you tell me that I'm supposed to break free from the whole New York Princess thing, because you don't want me to be snobby and spoiled, right?"

"Yes," she says softly.

"Then don't you think, maybe, you should have taught me more about everyone here? You could have shown me that life exists outside of New York. But, no you didn't. You let me believe the sun rose and set on 5th Avenue. You made me believe that I was the center of that universe,"

"I'm sorry." She looks at me and I look at her. We are standing in the space that used to be her space when she was my age. I wonder if Gram Tweety ever stood here with Mom. Talking about life. Did Gram and Gramps even know that Mom wanted to move to New York? Did they know she wanted to go to Law School and create an entirely new persona for herself? Did they know she'd laugh at parties and make fun of the backwards rednecks in the red states? Did they know she'd lose her accent and pull her hair back and be poised and safe and let her husband diminish her light?

I'm suddenly saddened by the thought of Mom at my age, standing in this very spot, trying so desperately to escape her life here that she'd literally become someone else.

"Why did you run away? What happened to you that made you want to leave this place?"

Mom just looks at me and blinks.

Ah. I know that trick. One I've used a thousand times. The deny-face. The hold-a-straight-face and blink and pretend you're not here face.

"Don't pull that shit with me MOM! I invented the blink and stare." I look at her and bat my eyes. The corners of her mouth curl up.

"No fooling you," she says and walks out of the bathroom. She crawls onto my bed and lays down.

"Nope. No fooling me," I say and follow her. "Seriously Mom. I just don't get you."

"You aren't entirely wrong Rian. Something did happen. I'm just trying to decide how much of it is necessary to tell you." She rolls over and props herself up on one arm.

"Don't play lawyer with me. I'm not a judge and jury. I'm not here to convict you or increase your child support," I tease.

"Yeah I know." She unceremoniously tugs at the fabric of her gray shirt, pulling it over her hip. I can tell she's deciding what to tell me and what to keep locked away in her heart.

"Well?"

"Well, Rian, the thing is..." her voice is already shaky. God is she going to cry? It's too early for this. "Gram Tweety and Gramps... you didn't know them. But, when I tell you they were good people, I mean it. They were the best kind of folks you could possibly know. They loved everyone in the Everglades and everyone loved them back. They were real old fashioned and they'd do anything for anyone, especially their own kin folk. Well, see, me and Aunt Kris. We weren't their real daughters. We were their granddaughters, they adopted us."

"What? Are you fucking kidding me?" I am shocked. I put my hands on my hips and pace around the room a few times. That was not what I was expecting Mom to say.

"Come sit down." She sits up and pats the edge of my bed and I go over and sit down next to her. I feel like I'm two inches tall right now.

"So who were your parents?"

Mom clears her throat. "Aunt Kris and I are the daughters of Gram and Gramps' only child. Her name was Samantha. Samantha was, um, how to put this–" Mom pauses and thinks about it for a moment. "She was like this beautiful, wild, exotic animal. Gram Tweety always wanted a daughter to raise in this house, to be a real Southern Belle. But Samantha was, I guess you'd say she was spoiled rotten. She did whatever she wanted without any fear of repercussions." Mom pats my knee and I get up and walk to my closet to pick my bathrobe up off the floor. I hang it on the hook in the bathroom before I come back to sit down.

Mom gives me a little nudge, like she's glad I came back to hear the rest of the story. "Samantha had Aunt Kris when she was sixteen and me at seventeen. I guess she decided two babies was too much for her to handle. So she left us here one day and never came back. The rumor was she wanted to be a movie star, not a teen mom in the Everglades."

"Mom, that's terrible! I'm so sorry," I say. Because, damn that really is a horrible start to life. Being abandoned by your birth mother. As if Mom and Aunt Kris meant nothing to her at all.

"That's not the only thing she did when she left."

"There's more?" I'm shocked all over again. What was it this time? Grand theft auto?

"Gramps fishing lure business was really starting to take off. He'd just built the big factory in town, and they were starting to make a name in the industry and some good money. Samantha knew Gram Tweety had been putting aside all their profits to restore this house and the lands. I mean, you saw that old picture, this place honestly wasn't much better than that when I was a kid."

Oh no. Not grand theft auto. Grand theft fishing lure money.

"She stole about two-hundred thousand dollars from Gram and Gramps. Then she left town, never to be seen in the Everglades again. It tore everyone apart. From what I've heard, Gram Tweety was never really the same. Mrs. Day helped out a lot, and all the people that worked here, they helped raise me and Aunt Kris. Gramps spent day and night at the factory avoiding his feelings. It wasn't the easiest kind of life for any of us after Samantha left."

"Jesus Mom. I mean, that's like some crazy shit. Are you okay? I mean, how did you find out about your Mom, I mean, how old were you when you realized Gram and Gramps weren't your birth parents?" I am in such utter disbelief. I mean, mom never talked about her parents or family life much. But, this is still insane to me!

"I was about a year old and Aunt Kris was two when Samantha left us here. Gram and Gramps didn't hide it from us. Her pictures are still on the wall. Her name wasn't off limits or anything. Which made it more like a wound that refused to heal. I could never understand why someone like Samantha, who had parents that gave her the world and had this entire town eating out of her hand, would just up and run away."

I feel sick to my stomach.

And Mom still isn't done talking.

"When I was about your age, I started looking for Samantha. I mean, it was the early 90's by then, and communication was getting easier and I was smart. That's how I ended up in New York. I was following a lead on Samantha and stayed to attend NYU and decided to put this part of my life behind me. Then I met your dad when I was in Law School."

I am in shock... utter and complete shock. I mean, first of all, this is the longest conversation I've had with Mom since, well, before her and Dad's divorce. I want to know more. I want to keep talking and learning about what happened when Mom chased after Samantha in New York. But, my wrist buzzes. It's Justine. It's already 9:30! I'm so late. But, how can I leave Mom when she's just poured her heart out to me?

This massive revelation about who she is.

Why she left Florida.

"Go. It's fine. I know you're going shopping with Justine."

I give her a look.

"What? Haven't you learned, us Southerners like to gossip. Go. Have fun shopping," Mom says as she slides off my bed in a graceful sort of way. She pulls one of her legs up into a tree pose and then does a neck roll. "I think I'll see if Darcy wants to do some yoga in the garden before we head back into the warehouse. You know, we've already found several ways to improve production on the fishing lures. Did your cousins tell you much about the family business?"

You've got to give it to Mom. She's the queen of misdirection and changing the subject in a way that makes you just as interested in the next thing she has to say that you completely forget what your original conversation was about.

I point a finger at her while I slip my feet into my shoes. "Don't do your lawyer shit on me, the misdirection, *I know you better than anyone.* This conversation about you and Samantha and what happened when you went to New York isn't over. It's just paused for a shopping break. And I'm using my Amex Platinum. So beware!" I tease and grab my Louis clutch and phone before rushing out of my room. But, as I run through the hallway full of old pictures staring at me, I realize I don't know Mom better than anyone.

I don't know her at all.

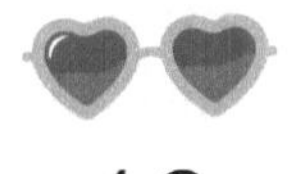

19

BRUNCH

I RUN OUT THE front door of the house and see an old red car in the driveway. Justine is in the driver's seat and the windows are rolled down. She's looking at her phone, but sees me from the corner of her eye and turns to bark at me. "Girl, I said nine. It's like–"

"Shut up and drive." I get into the passenger seat in a hurry.

"Don't slam–" she says as I slam the door shut.

"Oh, sor-ry." It comes out snotty and childish.

"God, what's up your ass? You'll be lucky if that door opens when we get there." She puts her foot on the gas and punches it. We sail down the driveway. Gravel flies up behind the tires, I can hear it plinking against the ancient metal of the old car. The window is already rolled down so I put my hand out and let the warm air glide through my fingers as we race down Old Palmetto Drive.

"Rian, I mean, I know you're kind of salty all the time, but seriously," Justine's voice is cool and I look over at her.

"Sorry," I say sweetly to smooth things over. "I was just with my Mom, she told me some, nevermind, it doesn't matter. I am sorry for being late." I don't really want to discuss the Samantha thing with Justine.

She gives me a look.

"Rian," her tone, it's supposed to make me tell her, but instead it makes me remember my dream last night. We were lying in the loft of the barn in a pile of hay and watching the stars out the big window. And then we did something that would have made the stars blush. I suck in a deep breath of the humid air and I can almost smell the hay. I smirk and shiver as chills go up my spine.

"I love your top," I say instead of divulging anything else about me and Mom's conversation. But, I mean it, about loving her top. She's wearing a tight bleached out vintage denim vest and I can see her collar bone showing. Something about seeing her skin and that delicate spot between her neck and chest makes me want to tell her to pull this stupid car over so I can crawl over the center console onto her lap and kiss her hard and hold her face in my hands.

"Thanks." Is all she replies before putting on her Ray-Bans. She reaches her hand over to turn up the music. I sink back into the seat and sing along and let the miles pass without saying anything else. She seems content to just drive and listen to music. But, it's giving me too much time to think about what Mom told me. I wonder if Sam and Travis know about Samantha? I mean, Sam is probably named after her. Which is kind of sadistic if you think about it. I wonder why Aunt Kris would do that to herself?

I glance over at Justine a few times. I wish she'd say something. Her eyes are glued to the road. Well, her sunglasses are. I can't really see what she's actually looking at. God I hope it's me. So much shit has happened and all I want to do is live life in this moment, right here, right now, with this girl next to me. This beautiful creature that I literally know nothing about. Except she loves vintage. She dresses to torment me. She doesn't take my shit. And apparently she likes shopping at trashy strip mall stores. Because as far as I know, there isn't anywhere else to shop in a 100 mile radius of where we live, except for that little place along the interstate, when I woke up briefly on our drive here because mom screamed, "LOOK RIAN, the Bealls Outlet!"

I did not look.

I did not care.

"Sam said you're not going to college," I say to break up the silence.

"Not for me." She laughs. I don't blame her, I don't think going to college is for me either, but I guarantee Mom will have other ideas.

"I want to go to–" but I stop myself from finishing that sentence. What's the point of telling her I want to go back to New York and go to art school? It's not like anyone cares about my art, or the stories I want to tell with it.

She glances over at me a few times, maybe thinking I'll tell her the rest of that sentence, but when I sink back into my seat and sing along to the radio again, she just keeps her eyes on the road and taps the beat on the steering wheel. It doesn't feel awkward or uncomfortable, it actually feels safe and relaxing not talking with her.

Just when I think we must have gone far enough, she flips on a blinker and makes a hard right turn into a parking lot filled with mini-vans and rusted trucks. There's one long row of discount stores with neon-signs blinking dully in the mid-morning sunshine.

"Don't embarrass me," she says after she parks before getting out.

"Excuse me?"

My door does open, despite her bitching at me about slamming it, so I get out and wiggle my dress down, since it's hiked up. Justine walks around to my side of the car and stands inches from me. I'm taller at this moment, only because I'm wearing wedges. Yeah, yeah, I know they aren't in style. But, I figure no one here will notice. I can smell her, she's so close, she smells like the mint plant growing in her bungalow mixed with rose oil. It's intoxicating. And for a split second I think she's going to hug me or kiss me and I freeze, because I'm not expecting it right here in this parking lot. But, instead she leans around me and uses her key to lock the car from the outside.

"The lock on my side is broken," she says. Her body brushes against me and my body tingles from the touch. "I'm starved. Let's have brunch." Justine turns and points to a silver diner with glass plate windows built right into the strip mall.

"Yeah, I could go for brunch," I say and follow her to the entrance. She opens the door for me with a smile.

"Ladies first." She motions me in. And I want to giggle, but I stop myself. Don't be an idiot!

The old lady at the front hands us menus and tells us to seat ourselves. Justine grabs them without a thank-you and strolls to a booth in the back, like she's been here before. She's got that personality. How I used to be in New York with my girls. When a place is your town, your home, you own it. You walk in with your head held high and demand to be seen.

The menu is a one page piece of laminated plastic. Justine doesn't even look at it. She's staring at me. I'm doing my best not to stare right into her eyes. I glance between her and the menu. I can feel the blood pulsing fast and hard in the vein in my neck. I wonder if Justine can see it.

A dumpy girl in her twenties, with dirty hair pulled up into a top knot, and an apron tied twice around her middle, comes over to take our order. But, I don't really know what to eat. It's all fried-this and smothered-that. I'm embarrassed to order anything.

"Hey Tara, me and my friend will have coffee, bacon, eggs over medium and pancakes."

"Yeah okay Justine. You know Frank was asking bout y'all. Said Big Jackie ain't called since all that shit went down. You should tell him to call." Then she turns and walks away in no real hurry.

"What was that all about?" I lean in and whisper.

"Oh nothing." She waves her hand dismissively. "Frank is me and Jackie's uncle. He's married to Tara's oldest sister. Everyone in Everglades City and all these little roadside stops know each other," Justine explains.

I raise an eyebrow at her. I know there is more to that story. But, she didn't pry about me and Mom so, I won't pry now.

"You ordered for me." I try not to smile.

"Is that a problem?" She asks. Her hands are folded on top of the table.

"No, but how did you know that's how I like my eggs?" I ask.

"I've been in the kitchen during breakfast... You barge in with your hair sloppy, in your booty shorts and tiny tank, complaining about scrambled eggs, wondering why they don't make them over medium. Then you take a biscuit or a muffin and stomp back to your room." She looks at me again, that stare. Like she's uncovered some secret truth about me because of the kind of eggs I like.

There's always so many people in the kitchen carrying on, especially in the mornings. I guess I didn't realize Justine was part of that mess. God how embarrassing. I'll have to make sure I fix my hair and get dressed before I go to the kitchen tomorrow.

"My pajamas aren't that bad," I whine.

Justine lets out a laugh. "I didn't say they were bad." Then those eyes again. I could get lost in them. Heat rises in my face just as Tara comes back and sets the coffee down. I don't usually drink black coffee. But, I watch as Justine blows the steam and sips it. I can tell she likes it. I take a sip. God it tastes awful. I try not to make a face, but from the look on hers, she can tell I'm not a fan.

"What would you have ordered?" She asks. Her lips curl up on the sides. Like she's waiting for me to say something off the wall.

"A mint mocha."

"Not a Starbucks for a hundred miles." She grins.

"Yeah, well they sell espresso machines. I mean, how hard is it to put chocolate and mint syrup into some milk and espresso?" I ask.

Her laugh is just right. It makes her eyes light up. She's got gold glitter eyeshadow on and perfect eye liner. How did I miss that before? Ava always says that glitter in eyeshadow means it's cheap. But, I don't give a damn, because it is so breathtaking on Justine.

She shakes her head. "You got so much to learn about this place."

I turn my head and gaze out the window. Then the breath in my lungs hisses out like a pressure valve slowly opening. "Everyone keeps saying that to me. But, why? Why do I have to learn about this place? I mean, I know, I get it, it's my home for now. But, as soon as I'm done with high school I'm going back to New York," I tell her and take another sip of the coffee. Still gross.

She frowns. Like going back to New York wasn't what she thought I might say. There is a flash of sadness on her face that makes my heart ache; I want to do something to make her smile again. I pull a pen out of my clutch and grab my napkin.

"What are you doing?" she asks.

"Hold still," I tell her. I glance back and forth from her to the napkin a few times and sketch her, the way she looks when she doesn't know I'm watching her. It's not my best work, but it's pretty good for pen-on-napkin. I turn it to show her.

"Oh my god! Did you draw that?" Tara is back with the food. It's steaming hot and piled high.

"Mind your own fucking business Tara." Justine snatches the napkin out of my hand and puts it on the seat next to her. I'm scared that I embarrassed her and we don't say much while we eat. We just look at each other occasionally. It's intense. I've never silently eaten at a table with someone who made me feel like this before.

Like, I want to pour my heart and soul out to her.

I want to sit on her couch with my head in her lap. I want her to play with my hair. I want to tell her about my life and being a spoiled New York Princess, but how underneath that facade I actually have some depth to me that no one else knows. Like, that I love to go to Central Park in the fall and sketch the leaves changing colors. Or that I love old black and white movies and singing in the bathtub. I want her to tell me she thinks I'm special. And then I'll sit up and pull her close to me and I'll tell her she's the special one, she's as unique and breathtaking as a snowflake and then we will laugh because she's never seen snow in real life before.

Then she'll kiss me. The kind of kiss that takes your breath away.

And I'll hold her tight to me.

We'll plan to go to New York together when I finish high school and turn eighteen. I'll buy her a winter coat, with a fur collar, and we will walk through the city in the snow and her eyes will light up and I'll tell her she's mine forever. While we wait for New York, we'll take long walks everyday holding hands. She'll tell me her dreams as we stroll through the fields and down Old Palmetto Drive. Our touch will be the one thing that keeps us grounded, because being together makes us feel so high.

Mom will say she's proud of me for finally letting someone in. Darcy will get weepy and say she always knew I would find someone to fall in love with who would understand me, the real me, the person I keep hidden away. Sam and Travis will think we are so cute together, but they'll be jealous of how much time I spend with Justine. So, I'll have to help them find girlfriends.

"Earth to Rian." Justine waves her hand in front of my face.

"Sorry," I mumble and put another bite of pancake in my mouth.

"I never met someone like you before," she says.

I feel her hand under the table gently touch my leg. It's enough to send my entire body into shock. I try not to choke on my pancake.

"I'm an original," I manage to reply after I swallow.

That makes her laugh and her hand squeezes my thigh. Before it can go anywhere else, Tara comes back over, and completely kills the mood.

"You done? My shift is over. Here's the check. Justine, don't forget to tell Jackie to call Frank," she puts a ticket on the table.

"Yeah, okay," Justine removes her hand from my leg and I frown. She slides out of the booth and walks up to pay for our breakfast. I'm not ready for this moment to be over! I let out a long sigh.

20

SHOPPING 101

AFTER OUR BRUNCH AT the diner, we cross the parking lot of the strip mall, under the blazing mid-day sun, and walk into the outlet store. As soon as we get inside, I sniff the air and look around. New York stores smell like clean laundry and money. But the air here smells like trash and farts. I have a moment of panic when I see the orange shopping carts and hear someone saying there is a blue dot special over the intercom system.

Justine doesn't seem to notice. "I'm looking for something. Shoes are over on those racks," she says before heading off on her own.

"Don't puke, don't puke."

I force the pancakes back down into my stomach. I never in a million years expected to shop in a place like this. I don't know what to do. I'm used to shopping in boutiques with private rooms where me and the NYP's can view models showing off the latest styles from the runways of Milan, Italy. We get offered sparkling water and champagne.

This store has horrible, overhead fluorescent lights and rows of clothes, racks of shoes, cheap holiday decorations, pictures, and even furniture for sale crammed into every crevice.

I close my eyes for a second, to calm down.

I imagine when Gina and I used to sneak off to vintage shops in SoHo behind Ava's back. Those were some of my favorite shopping expeditions in the city. The quaint and unique things I'd find, the chill ambiance, the smell of vintage. If I can pretend this is one of those vintage shops in New York, maybe I'll survive. But when I open my eyes, nope. Still a crappy outlet store with a heavy stench of body odor.

"Shoes."

I told Darcy I'd find her shoes. That's what I have to do. If I have something to look for to take my mind off the horror of discount shopping in the Everglades, I will survive. I try not to let my eyes dart around for Justine. She said she was looking for something and seemed secretive about it. Apparently she doesn't know girl code; shopping is meant to be done in pairs.

I guess I'll need to teach her the basics. Shopping 101.

I reach the aisle of shoes. They are stacked practically on top of each other in various colored shoe boxes on big metal racks. They are mismatched and shoved in with no rhyme or reason. There are athletic shoes next to pumps. Flip-flops by rows of snow boots. Why the hell are there snow boots in South Florida? But, after a bit of searching, I manage to find a few pairs of simple, leather strap sandals in a size ten. Nothing fancy, but they are classic and will go with anything Darcy wears. I grab them out of their boxes and walk down the row to the other side.

"Now what," I mumble.

"Now you try this on," Justine whispers in my ear.

She's right behind me. I didn't even see her creep up on me. Chills go up my spine and I turn around. We are pressed chest to chest. Can she feel my heart beating?

"Come with me to the dressing room." She grabs my hand and drags me to the back of the store. I can't see what she wants me to try on. But, right now, the way I feel, I don't care if it's a chicken suit, I would follow this girl anywhere. She literally takes my breath away.

"Justine, what are you up to?" I laugh.

"You need clothes for fishing and mudding." She opens a dressing room stall and pushes me in. "Try these on. And show me."

"I, uh, okay," I stumble on the words as I stumble into the dressing room. Remind me again why I wore wedges? She laughs and closes the door.

I put my hand on the metal lock and press my forehead to the door of the dressing room. She's on the other side of this door waiting for me. Ten minutes ago I wouldn't have been caught dead trying on anything from this place and now I can't wait to see what Justine wants me to wear. The dressing room is tiny, with orange laminate walls and a floor-to-ceiling mirror that's warped and makes my ass look huge and my head look small. I manage to get my dress off and slide on a pair of green shorts and one of the tanks from the things she picked out. I don't look at myself in the freakshow mirror, instead I open the door and look at Justine.

She steps closer to me.

I took my shoes off to change, so she's taller, only by an inch, but it gives her the edge she needs. She puts her hands on my waist and feels around the fabric of the shorts and oh my god, I think my knees are knocking together.

"These are too loose. You have such a narrow waist. I'll grab you a smaller size. But, the tank looks good on you. Do you like it?"

"If you think it looks good on me, then I like it." I smile. For the first time in, I don't know when, I could care less what I look like or what kind of cheap fabric is rubbing against my skin. "Justine, do you have a boyfriend?" I have to ask. I don't want to misread what I think is happening between us. Because this might be how girls act in the swamp. But in New York, this means something else entirely. This means that feeling I have, that tingle, that spark, that–

She laughs.

"What?" I frown.

"Do *you* think I have a boyfriend?" She reaches up and tucks a piece of my hair behind my ear. Her fingers stroke my cheek.

"No, I don't." I lean into her hand and close my eyes. Her touch is making me tremble. "Kiss me Justine," I whisper.

But instead of kissing me, she says, "I'm gonna grab you a pair of smaller shorts."

I open my eyes. My lips are pouty and slightly parted, I mean, I thought this was heading in that direction. The way she touched me, under the table during brunch and just now, on the cheek. Could I have been so wrong? She's shaking her head as she walks away.

Like I'm a big fucking joke.

I lock the door to the changing room.

Oh my god. How embarrassing. I threw myself at her and she rejected me. I change my clothes quickly, grab the stupid shoes for Darcy and the rest of the clothes Justine picked out for me, and race to the register. I slam it all down on the counter.

"Well, now, look at all these goodies," says the woman behind the register. "Look here, Trish, don't this pretty little thing look like something from a fashion magazine!" She tugs the orange vest on the woman behind her who's checking out someone else. The woman turns around and looks at me and at the pile of stuff I slammed on the counter.

"You're right! You are so precious. Where you get that dress you got on? I know it ain't one of ours. You get that someplace round here? Or online?"

"New York." I huff. I am not in the mood for this.

"NEW YORK?" both women practically scream at the same time.

"We gotta go ladies, if you don't mind," Justine puts her arm around me from behind, like nothing is wrong. Like I mean something to her. Like she didn't just walk away from me when I asked her to kiss me. She places the smaller pair of green shorts on the pile of clothes. "She'll take these ones too."

Trish's eyes get big and she spins back to her customer. The woman helping me, who's name tag says

"Patti" puts her head down and rings up my stuff. "If you say so," she mumbles and scans the tag.

"I'll be in the car." Justine squeezes me once before strolling out the double doors. I watch her walk away, every inch of her, my cheeks are flushed. I'm struggling to figure her out– does she like me or not? This is torture!

"You know her?" Patti interrupts my mental anguish.

"Yeah, obviously. Why? Do you know her?" I ask and narrow my eyes at the woman.

"Of course we know her!" Trish finishes with her customer and looks at me and Patti who fumbles with the hangers.

"That's the one who killed her stepdaddy," Patti replies, her big, wide-set eyes staring at me.

"The paper said it was a murder-suicide, but we all know what really happened. You be careful round that one." Trish tilts her head and nods toward the parking lot. Toward Justine.

"Just shut the fuck up and tell me how much I owe for all this crap."

They both look at me.

Heads shaking.

21

Get Away from Me

"So, were you or Sam or Travis or ANYONE at the fucking bullshit manor going to tell me you murdered Uncle Chuck?" I'm so angry I can't see straight.

"Don't slam–"

But, I slam the door, and it makes a weird click-bang when it latches. I don't care if I just broke her stupid, junky old car.

"Well, now you've done it. That door won't open again until I take off the panel and unhook the pins. I told you not to slam it." Justine turns up the air conditioning after she revs the engine. But, I'm so mad I hardly feel the change in temperature. She pulls out of the parking lot acting like I've said nothing. She just smiles.

"Well, aren't you going to say something?" I turn and look at her. "Anything?"

"Did you know this was your Mom's car? It's a 1992 Limited Edition Ford Mustang. She only had it for a year before she ran off to New York, chasing Samantha. It sat in the barn under a cover until your Aunt Kris let me have it when I was fourteen. I put in all the work to restore it." She pauses and wipes some imaginary crumb from her lip and glances at me. "Yeah, okay, my brother Jackie helped, some."

My brain races in circles trying to cope with what I just heard. So, not only are people saying Justine murdered Uncle Chuck, but she knows about Samantha? And she openly talks about her as if her existence wasn't this huge secret my Mom kept from me for sixteen years.

"Goddamnit Justine!" I slam my hands on the dash as I shriek.

"Calm down." Her knuckles turn white as she grips the steering wheel.

"Why should I calm down? I mean. What the hell? Did you kill Uncle Chuck? And what really happened to Aunt Kris?" I'm losing my mind over here and start sucking in short, fast breaths.

"That monster had it coming. But, it wasn't me. Why don't you ask Sam and Travis what really happened." Then she reaches her hand out, and for a split second I think she's going to put it on my leg, to try and reassure me everything will be okay. All she does is turn up the music as loud as it can go. I don't argue with her anymore. She's letting me know she's done talking. She might not have killed Uncle Chuck, but she knows what really happened, and it involves Sam and Travis. My heart beats so fucking hard, I really might get sick. I close my eyes and pray we get back to Cullier Manor House as soon as possible.

Whatever romantic feelings I thought we had, I'm not sure they can survive the tension in this old car.

Justine pulls up and parks on the side of the Big House and gets out. Of course my door doesn't open, just like she said. So, I have to climb over the middle console and get out on her side. She doesn't help me, but runs off in the direction of her house because she wants to get away from me as fast as she can. Spiteful me leaves her door wide open with hopes it fills up with no-see-ums and mosquitoes. I don't take the bag of crap I bought at that disgusting outlet store and leave it sitting in the back seat. Darcy can buy her own fucking shoes and I will never wear anything Justine picked out for me.

I walk toward the front porch, ready to go inside and lock myself in my room, and never look at another person here again. But, of course, Sam and Travis come barreling outside before I even put my foot up on the step.

"RIAN! Perfect timing. We've got big plans—Travis saw a ten-foot gator out in the swamp last night. We're gonna go hunting." Sam is wearing his big rubber overalls and has a spear in one hand.

"Gators that big are trouble for the ecosystem. We've got to kill him," Travis says seriously.

Is that what really happened the night Uncle Chuck died?

Sam and Travis decided he was big trouble for the ecosystem of Cullier Manor House and they killed him? Then my poor Aunt Kris killed herself because she found out her sons were murderers? I hold my hand over my mouth.

"You okay, cous? You look like you're gonna be sick," Sam grimaces.

"Maybe you shouldn't come gator hunting with us. I have a strict no vomit on the boat policy." Travis inches away from me.

His rubber boots squeak like nails on a chalkboard. I shake my head and run into the house before either of them can say another word to me. I don't want to imagine my cousins as killers. I don't want to picture the tragedy that happened in this house.

"Hey, Rian!" It's Darcy in those heinous Birkenstocks coming out of the library and into the foyer. What cruelness is this?

"Piss off." I run up the stairs two at a time.

"So, that's the mood today?" she laughs, like it's some game.

Okay, so maybe back home in New York I used to be in a bad mood for no particular reason. But, today, I have a one-hundred percent legitimate reason for my foul mood. This is the real deal. This is an *I hate you* kind of mood. So, get out of my way or get ready for my wrath.

As soon as I get into my room I break down.

I kick off my stupid wedge shoes and crawl into my bed. The sheets and duvet are mine, but they aren't mine from back home, which makes me feel even worse. I roll over and pull them over me anyway and sob into my pillow. Like, uncontrollably sob.

My body shakes.

I can't stop thinking that my cousins are murderers. And my Mom had a mother who abandoned her and Aunt Kris. Or about my long-lost life in New York. And my Dad. Who by the way hasn't answered his fucking phone in so long I wonder if *he's still alive?*

I look at my phone, it's dead. I reach for my charger but then remember I left it in the bathroom. UGH! I don't want to get up. I lean down and pull my Louis from under the bed, I know I have a spare charger in it somewhere.

"Lanie," I say when I move the American Girl doll out of the way to find the extra charger. Something about her plastic face and dumb toothy grin makes me feel comforted in a weird, childish way. So, I pull her into the bed with me and the extra charger. I plug my phone in, determined to call Dad and Heather until one of them answers.

While my phone charges, I curl into a ball and hold Lanie and continue to cry. I made a fool of myself today. First, I practically threw myself at Justine in that dressing room asking her for a kiss and ten minutes later I accused her of murder! I just want to know what the hell is going on around here because there are way too many secrets. If Mom and Sam and Travis and Justine would all be honest with me, none of this would have happened. Is it because they are worried how I'll react? Or do they think I'm not worthy of knowing things? Am I that much of a spoiled brat? Am I really so terrible?

I scream.

Even if they hear me screaming downstairs, no one comes to check on me. I've built walls with expensive clothes and a princess attitude. But, what if I don't want to be that Rian anymore?

What if something was really wrong—would anyone come and rescue me?

22

WHO KILLED UNCLE CHUCK?

I FALL ASLEEP WAITING for my phone to charge.

I dream about Justine. Her sun-kissed hair floating behind her as she runs through a swamp forest. She's a ghost, sort of fuzzy around the edges. I'm chasing after her, trying to keep up—but I can't reach her. She looks back at me with a smile and says, *Come on, Rian. Follow me.* I try, but the vines creep up from the swamp and wrap around my ankles. She's so fast, running between the palm trees and jumping over fallen rotted logs. *Wait for me*, I yell after her, but she disappears. The ground is muddy under my feet and little, black gator eyes pop out of the water on the edge of the forest, waiting for me to sink, waiting for me to fall.

JUSTINE! I cry out to her.

I wake up to the sound of voices outside my door. It's dark in my room, I must have slept all day and half the night. I wasn't even that tired, just emotionally drained. I find my phone on the edge of my bed and check the time.

2 a.m.

There's a knock.

It better not be Sam and Travis. I am not in the mood for their adventures right now.

"I'm coming, calm down." The glow of my phone is the only light as I tip-toe toward the door. I'm disoriented, my dream about Justine in the swamp felt so real. I open it a crack and peek out. It's Travis and he's wearing his cowboy hat. He only wears that stupid thing when he's up to no good. I can smell the beer on him.

"What's going on? Who were you talking to?" I swing the door open all the way and rub the sleep from my eyes. I look down at myself, still in my white dress from earlier.

"Ain't nobody but me out here. Sorry, did I wake you, cous?" he asks.

His words are slurred and he's unsteady on his feet. Where has he been tonight? I can't believe no one came to wake me for dinner. My stomach is growling and angry.

"I'm awake. What do you want?" I ask.

"You wanna take a drive?" He fumbles around in his pocket. He pulls out the keys to his truck and jingles them.

"No, and you're definitely not driving anywhere in your condition. Give me the keys, cowboy." I hold my hand out. I'm not going to let him kill himself in a drunk driving accident. He frowns, but drops them in my hand. Then he scoops me into a really awkward hug and picks me up off the ground. We wobble around until he sets me back down.

"God, Travis. How much did you drink tonight?"

"I dunno…"

"Come on, doofus. Let's put you to bed before my Mom finds you drunk and makes you take a cold shower." I push him out of my door frame and down the hall toward his bedroom.

"No, let's go to the kitchen. I'm starved."

I think about it for a minute. Food would be good for him, to help soak up the alcohol. And I am starving. So, I grab his hand and pull him along the hallway, then I put my arm around his waist so he doesn't tumble down the stairs and wake everyone up.

"You been hiding all day, missed the gator hunt. Big fella got away," he slurs and flops himself on a chair when we reach the kitchen.

I open the fridge and take out some containers of random leftovers, broccoli salad, fried chicken, and some kind of shrimp. I go to the pantry and pull out a bag of potato chips and some chocolate chip cookies.

"Mmmm… you're a good cook," Travis says with a mouthful of chicken leg and a handful of chips.

"Oh, you can't be that drunk." I laugh for the first time in what feels like forever. "I didn't make any of this." But, he doesn't seem to care or notice as he shovels a handful of broccoli salad into his mouth, without a fork or anything. Yuck. Boys are so gross!

I go over to the cabinet on the other side of the kitchen and mix myself a vodka and cranberry juice. Mom's gonna freak out if she finds us down here eating in the middle of the night and Travis in his drunken state, so I might as well sneak a drink. As I sip on my drink and eat three of the big, chocolate chip cookies as I stare at Travis. I feel terribly guilty for thinking he could have been involved in his parents' deaths.

Look at him. Just a dumb, sappy, country boy.

I bet this is what he does on Friday nights; sits in his shop listening to music and drinking beers. Or maybe he was feeling sad and drank to drown his sorrows.

"Is everything okay, Travis?" I decide to ask.

"You made Justine cry." Travis puts down his food and looks me in the eye. I'm taken aback and nearly choke on my drink. "That ain't cool, cous. She's like family to me. You ain't allowed to make her cry."

"Wait, what? Why was she crying?" I'm confused and set down my drink. "I'm the one who threw myself at her, asking for a kiss, and she rejected me. And then when I confronted her about what the clerk at the store said, she got mad and ignored me the entire drive home. I'm the one who was crying." I fold my arms over my chest waiting for Travis to apologize. I can't believe Justine came home and cried to my cousin about me.

"Did you say y'all almost kissed? You and Justine?" Now Travis is the one who is confused.

"Yes we almost kissed," I snap. "I don't know what she told you, but obviously it was only half of what really happened." I'm super annoyed now. I just want to go back to bed.

"Why are you mad at me?" he slurs.

I let out a long sigh. He's too drunk to understand me and Justine. I'm not sure I understand me and Justine. "You should go to bed now, Come on, I'll help you up the stairs." I put my arm under him and lift him from the seat in the kitchen and drag him back upstairs to his room. I've never been in his room. Or Sam's either. I guess, I figure their space is private. Travis is like a wobbly toddler as we navigate through the doorway and walk toward his bed.

Even though I'm sort of annoyed because he's a handful right now, I am glad he came to my room tonight. He might have done something really stupid if I hadn't stopped him from driving. I don't think Mom or Sam would survive if something bad happened to Travis.

"Thanks, Rian," his voice is soft and sleepy. It reminds me of the time Ava got so smashed at her Grandma's house in the Hamptons I had to hold her hair back all night while she puked, then I carried her to bed around 4 a.m. and stayed wrapped around her to make sure she kept breathing.

"You aren't going to be sick or anything right? Like, you don't need me to stay or something..." I take the cowboy hat off his head and put it on top of the lamp next to his bed and look around. His room is clean and it smells like him. There are posters of hotrods up on the walls and trophies from kid's sports teams. He has a desk with a computer and some video games. There is a big world map with places circled and x'd out. Maybe places he wants to go?

"Travis?" I turn and look at him because he never answered me. He's curled up on his bed crying into a pillow. "Travis, cous, hey are you okay?" I gently shake his shoulder.

"No, I'm not fucking okay, Rian. I'm a wreck."

I don't know what I should do. Should I stay? Should I leave? Some people are really private about their grief.

"Do you want me to go?" I ask tenderly.

"Please, don't go." He sits up and reaches his hand out to me and grabs my wrist. I'm surprised by the grip of his hand, and sit down on the edge of his bed.

"You miss them?" I ask.

"I miss *her.*" He sobs like a little boy for his Mama.

I want to say more, you know, something profound to make him feel better and make sense of what happened in this house. But ever since I arrived, we've all avoided the conversation of what really happened.

Tears stream down my face, hot and salty on my skin.

"What really happened to your parents?" I finally work up the nerve to ask Travis between my sniffles. The light from the side lamp makes shadows on the walls. I stare at them, and after what feels like forever, he squeezes my hand.

"You really wanna know?"

"No," I reply. My heart pounds. I'm scared to turn and look at him. "But, I think you'll feel better if you talk about it." The ghosts who wander these halls... They are listening. Anxious to know if this is the story that might set their soul free, to pass to the other side. I feel their presence; a thickness and weight in the air.

Do I really want to know all the gruesome details about what happened here? I feel like I'm going to be sick. Travis takes a deep breath, as if he's preparing to get all of this off of his chest, once and for all.

"Daddy wasn't a good man. He hurt us, all of us." Travis looks around the room. I wonder if he too senses the ghosts. "Lotta beatings when we was little, you know. But then he started using the belt, and then his fists. Mama took as much as she could to keep him from coming after me and Sam all the time."

"Oh, Travis, I'm so sorry." I can't imagine being a child and enduring that kind of abuse, but something about what he said, with the belt, it's familiar. It jogs a memory loose, one I had buried deep. "That's why my Dad hated him."

It was after our one and only family vacation, I sketched two boys crouched in a corner of a hotel room with a man and a belt in his hand. Dad screamed and snatched the picture away from me. He scared me, *just like Uncle Chuck*. I remember Mom and Dad arguing and Dad saying we would never see that redneck child beater again. That's why Mom sobbed and cried after our trip and why Dad hated it here. It was because of Uncle Chuck.

"Daddy wasn't a good man," Travis says again and curls back up on the bed.

"Men who beat their kids and wives are pieces of shit." My tears are replaced with anger. Travis moans. "You didn't do anything wrong, Travis," I say and pull him toward me. "You didn't deserve it. You hear me. You didn't deserve it." I try to comfort him.

"I did something bad," he says and pulls away from me.

"No, you didn't do anything wrong." But my heart starts pounding because I'm beginning to get the feeling there really is more to the story.

"Everyone in town knew he was a monster. It wasn't just the beatings. He gambled and drank and cheated on Mama. I'm so ashamed to be his son. She was finally going to leave him. She had the papers and everything. Had her suitcases packed." I can tell he's proud of his Mom for having that kind of strength, but his pride quickly turns back into tears. "That's why he choked the life out of her. He said she could never leave. Justine walked in, bringing Mama another bag, and caught him. She tried to stop it, so he tried to kill her too." He leaps from the bed, the moonlight slicing through the window, casting wicked shadows along the wall as he paces around the room like there is a monster over his shoulder. He rubs his face a few times and pushes his hair back, then looks at me. I shake with fear.

"Uncle Chuck tried to kill Justine?" I barely get the words out of my mouth.

"I don't know how she managed to get away, but she did. Justine is strong, she don't take shit from anyone. Including Daddy. He ran after her, through the house, screaming, and firing a gun."

"It was self-defense." I don't even have to hear the rest of the story. They were being terrorized by Uncle Chuck. All of them. Every person in this house was afraid for their life.

"I just came in from fishing and heard the gun going off. Justine was screaming at Daddy, calling him a piece of shit, sayin he killed Mama. He had her backed into a corner with the gun in her face. I tackled him to the floor, but he wouldn't stop. He still had the gun."

I rock back and forth on the bed. My hands over my mouth

"Oh, Travis." I mumble. "Oh god." I squeeze my eyes shut and shake my head. I'm in shock. At least, I think that's what this feeling must be. Because my hands go cold and my throat dry.

"I don't really know how it happened, there was a struggle, and the gun went off. His blood was all over me and Justine. It was everywhere, I— I— Uh–"

Then he vomits on the floor, wiping his face with his sleeve, and looking at me. Those crystal, clear blue eyes are dark with shame. Is he saying what I think he's saying? Did he pull the trigger?

"If you killed him, it was self-defense, Travis. My mom can explain it to a judge." I'm certain of it. If Uncle Chuck was running around the house like a madman, shooting a gun, had just killed Aunt Kris, and had Justine backed into a corner, Travis had to stop him.

"*He* was holding the gun, Rian. It wasn't in my hand. I'm not in any trouble... The police came and they called it suicide. But, I don't know! I just don't know!"

Travis falls to his knees and heaves again. There's nothing left to come out and I am in such a state of panic I get up and run out of the room.

Knock, knock.

I don't wait for Sam to answer. I barge into his room. I must have scared the shit out of him, because he jumps out of bed in nothing but his boxer shorts and a t-shirt, grabs a baseball bat and is ready to take my head clean off. His eyes are wild with adrenaline.

"It's just me! Put down the bat!" I hiss.

"Rian, you scared the—"

I throw my hands out. "Yeah, shut up. Look, Travis just told me what really happened that night with your parents." My lips are numb and it's hard to form the words. "I can't stay with him right now. You need to take care of him. He's drunk and puking and I... I... " He doesn't hesitate. He puts down the bat and runs out of the room toward Travis. I follow him out, but turn the other way.

"Wait! Where are you going?" he asks me.

"I have to know who really killed Uncle Chuck."

Sam shouts something, but I'm already running down the stairs, taking them two at a time. The wood feels hard and unforgiving under my bare feet. I head for the front door and rush into the sticky night air. It's a weird time, almost morning, but not. The moon is gone and dew is trying to form.

I have to know the truth.

I have to find Justine.

23

PANTHER VS. ALLIGATOR

I KNOCK ON THE door of Justine's house but there's no answer. I'm breathing heavily and feel like puking, I need her right now, but I'm scared to knock harder. What if she's the kind of girl who gets super pissed off when someone wakes her up when it's still dark out? What am I even going to say? *Did Travis pull the trigger? Did you?* She already refused to tell me what when I asked her about it earlier today and told me to ask Sam and Travis.

Does it really matter who killed Uncle Chuck?

He was the worst kind of man, a child beater, a drunk, a cheat. Not to mention he killed Aunt Kris. And Travis said the police ruled it a suicide, so that should be the end of story.

Justine isn't coming to the door, so I decided maybe I'll just sit down on the porch and wait for the sun to come up. I can't go back and face Travis or Sam or Mom or Darcy or anyone else in the house right now. I lean my head up against Justine's door and close my eyes. But I can't keep them closed. I know it shouldn't matter who pulled the trigger... Uncle Chuck was a piece of shit.

But something about it, it eats at me.

God, Justine was right... *I'm a teen detective.* I think if I knew what really happened–if Travis knew for certain it wasn't him, he might be able to live with it. Because right now he's scared. He's scared that during the scuffle, he's the one who pulled the trigger and somehow put the gun in Uncle Chuck's hand.

He doesn't want to be a murderer–even though Uncle Chuck deserved it.

I still have my smart watch on and text Ava. Then Dad.

After five minutes neither of them have answered. I'm not surprised by Ava, it's Friday in NYC. She's probably passed out at Gina's house after going clubbing. But Dad. There's no reason why he can't answer his phone in Germany. It's the middle of the day there. What could be more important than talking to me when I text him that it's an emergency and *I need him.*

It's starting to feel like I'm the one with a dead dad.

After ten minutes of sitting outside Justine's house, I'm so anxious I can't stand it. I start tapping my fingers on my leg. If I had my sketch pad, maybe I could draw and get out some of my feelings. But, like I said, I'm not going back into the house. After a few more minutes I stand because there is no way I can sit here until the sun comes up, I will go crazy. I've been on an emotional rollercoaster and the adrenaline in my system is screaming to get out.

I pace around at first, up and down by the shop, kicking the heads off flowers. Then I see that red muscle car, the one Travis was fixing the first day we got here. Uncle Chuck's car. I remember how defensive Travis was—but the more I think about it, it's because he was scared of what had happened. How can I blame him? I have to get out of here, away from everything. I start running even though I'm barefoot. I push myself harder and faster than I ever have before. Which is totally insane because I've never been on this side of the property and I have no idea where I'm going. And I hate running. Especially barefoot in a dress.

I'm being stupid.

This is so stupid! But I can't stop. I keep running and sucking in the muggy swamp air.

Run.

Breathe.

Run.

Breathe.

I'm going to run into that fucking skunk or a wild boar, which Sam says are cute but dangerous. But I can't stop myself. If I stop, I'll only think about what happened to my cousins and my Aunt. They spent their lives being terrorized by Uncle Chuck.

It really makes my temper tantrums about leaving New York seem completely insignificant. I'm embarrassed for every foul thing I said, every bad attitude, every spoiled and demanding action. My feet cry out in pain from the brush and palms and sticks. But, I can't stop myself.

The pain in my feet is nothing compared to what my family endured. That's why I keep running. Mom and Aunt Kris were abandoned by their teenage mom,

Samantha. A girl who dreamed of leaving this life behind. Then Mom did exactly the same thing, ran away to New York and never came back. And poor Aunt Kris, abandoned not once, but twice–stayed here to keep the family business going and provide a good life for Sam and Travis and Justine and all these people who loved and depended on her.

But, stupid, fucking, terrible Uncle Chuck.

He beat the joy from their lives. For what reason? They had money! They had a beautiful home! Everything someone could want! But Travis said he was a bad man. A gambler, a drunk, a cheater.

Why didn't Aunt Kris leave sooner?

I stop running and put my hands on my knees and pant. I know why she didn't leave. The same reason Mom didn't divorce Dad when she was unhappy.

Pride.

The deadliest of sins.

A sin I wear so well in my designer clothes. I wretch, but nothing comes out.

I look around, and I don't know where I am. A swampy forest like the one from my dream about Justine. I must be miles from the house by now. I ran for so long and nothing here looks familiar.

"Well, now what?"

I'm profusely sweating and completely out of breath. I lean against one of the oak trees and let the sounds of the Everglades sing me a song. I wish more than anything I could rewind today, just start over. But, where would I start over? This morning? Before Mom told me about

Samantha? Or before we moved here at all? Back in New York.

But, I love Sam and Travis. I know I've only been here for a few weeks, but I can't imagine my life without them.

I'm so sick over what happened to Aunt Kris and I wish she didn't have to die for me to get to know my cousins and everyone here at Cullier Manor House. I hate that Travis thinks he might have been the one to pull the trigger. I shake my head.

I need to go home and find Mom and tell her what happened. Maybe she already knows. Maybe that was part of why she rushed to move us here, to make sure she could protect Travis if the truth came out he was the one who pulled the trigger.

But what she doesn't know, what I need to tell her, is that I'm ready to be a part of this life. All of it. The messy parts. The happy parts. All of it. I want to be here for her and Darcy and Sam and Travis and Justine and everyone. I'm ready to grow up and ditch the New York Princess crown and focus on being a good daughter, a good cousin, a good person. Because I love this place, for all its faults and the pain that lingers, I love it here and I don't want to run away.

"You hear that swamp! I love this stupid fucking place even though you're terrorizing me tonight," I say out-loud.

There is a crackle in the brush near my feet. A twig snaps on a branch over my head reminding me I'm not alone. I'm in the middle of the Everglades and there are creatures everywhere. Sam proved that to me in the blind. This place is always alive. It is a city that never sleeps.

"Prrrrgggrr."

The hair on the back of my neck stands up and it works its way down my spine and arms. I've heard a sound like that before. My heart beats faster. I look up in the tangles of the tree branches and I see her.

A Florida panther.

The protective mother. A fighter. A beast. A creature who once looked me in the eye when I questioned everything I thought I knew, and she told me the answer. She welcomed me home. I didn't listen to her before. Maybe now she's here to get revenge on me because I have taken all of it for granted.

"I believe you. This is my home, I believe you," I whimper.

Tears roll down my cheeks. She moves her strong haunches, coming closer, and I'm a deer frozen with fear. I sniffle. I am not cut out for this... until about ten minutes ago I would have said I'm a New York Princess and should be out dancing with my friends or shopping for clothes or going to the Hamptons. But now, I want this life, and all the strings that are attached— the heartache, the hard work, all of it.

So, I do the only thing I can think of.

"Aunt Kris, if your ghost is here, please protect me from being eaten by the panther. I promise I'm going to be better. I'm going to help Travis cope with what happened." I put my hands up in the air like I'm praying, or begging. The wind rustles the leaves at my feet and I'm overwhelmed with the feeling of home. "I'm going to go to school with Sam and join teams and be his new BFF. I know they need me. I need them too. Please, you've got to understand. I wasn't ready when I got here, but I'm ready now. I'm ready for this life. I will be a good daughter. I will be a good friend. I'll go fishing every day and I'll work hard," I sob into the night.

The panther inches closer to me. I don't know where her baby is, but it's probably watching. Learning how to stalk prey and learning how to hunt. And I had the nerve to think it was cute. Now, it thinks I'm cute enough to eat. Oh, God. Holy Hell.

"I don't want to die," I beg. The panther perks up and makes a purring noise at me. I don't know if I should laugh or scream at this point.

Then, in the swamp water which isn't far behind me, I hear another noise. A hissing sound. Throaty and guttural. I don't recognize it at first. But the more I listen, the more it sounds like– oh fuck.

The panther is angling her body to jump.

"Rian, look out!" A woman's voice calls to me.

Then all hell breaks loose.

The panther leaps with one powerful swift movement and I turn to protect myself, but she's not leaping at me. Her body sails right by me, so close I feel her tan fur brush against my cheek. I spin and watch as she lands on a ten-foot alligator that is inches away from me with a wide open jaw. I scream bloody murder and fall forward on the ground, a stick pierces my leg, but I hardly feel the pain as I claw my way in the dirt to get away from the fight. The panther and alligator wrestle around hissing and growling and yelping and crying.

"HELP!" I scream. I scramble to my feet. "HELP!"

I don't want the panther to die. She's a mother. She just saved me from the alligator. I look around for whoever called my name, but I don't see anyone. I don't hear anyone calling for me again. I scream louder.

"HELP! STOP! STOP FIGHTING!"

I grab two sticks and smack them together, hoping to create a loud enough noise to frighten the two animals apart. But they don't even register the noise over the sounds of their fighting.

"Run," a voice says.

"But I can't leave her. What if she dies?" I cry, but I know I have to get out of here. They could decide to turn on me, they are wild creatures. Alpha predators. I'm nothing more than a piece of meat to them. My leg hurts when I start running in the direction I came from and I'm not sure any amount of adrenaline will keep me going.

But, somehow, I manage to move and run, stumbling in the palm brush and leaning against trees when I get tired. I keep falling down and slamming hard into the ground everytime I try to move. I know I have to keep going, despite the pain. I have to pick myself up and make it to the house. I'm nearly out of the swampy part and back to the field. I can see lights from the property calling me home.

"HELP!" I scream. "I'M HERE, HELP!" My throat is rough and cracked.

There's movement in the distance.

"RIAN!" Big Jackie shouts. He's running full speed toward me.

"Big Jackie," I gasp.

The tightness in my chest loosens when I see him. Lights begin flicking on at the Big House. Everyone is waking up to my screams for help. Person after person is rushing this direction, praying there hasn't been another tragedy.

24

I'M SORRY

BIG JACKIE REACHES ME in the field where I've collapsed next to a clump of dead grass. I'm covered in blood and sweat. My hands and feet and knees and legs are raw and sliced open wide from sticks and saw palmetto razor barbs. He scoops me up in one swift motion and I don't fight it.

"You've got to go save her. She attacked a ten-foot gator to save me. She's got a kitten. You've got to go help her!" I sob. I don't want that stupid cat to die. Sam said they are ultra rare and he was so happy the night we saw her in the blind. If she dies, I'll never be able to live with myself.

"Shhhh." He carries me back toward the house.

"NO!" I beat against his chest. "GO, you have to save her!"

"What the hell is going on out here?" Justine comes rushing outside as we pass her house. "Rian, oh my god, what happened to you?" She puts her hand up to my bloody face.

I'm still sobbing. I manage to squeak out the words panther and alligator.

"Come on, bring her inside my house," Justine orders her big brother. He doesn't argue and walks inside while Justine holds open the screen door. He carries me to Justine's bedroom and sets me down on her bed. "Go get Tori and tell Mrs. Day to put the coffee on. Get Sam and Travis. They better go see what's up in the swamp."

"No, Travis is drunk," I cry.

Justine and Big Jackie give each other a look.

"Rian, I'll go round the house and get your Mama and check on your cousins. You're safe now, let Justine fix you up." Big Jackie leaves the room in a hurry.

"Jesus, Rian. You look like shit." Justine's words might be harsh, but her voice is tender and concerned. Her eyes scan me quickly assessing the extent of my injuries. I can only imagine what my face looks like covered in swamp muck and mascara. My white dress is practically ripped clean off and what parts remain are covered in dried blood and mud. My hands and feet are throbbing and there are sticks and burs in my hair. While I'm feeling sorry for the state of myself, Justine moves around her place with purpose.

I watch, through swollen eyes, as she goes into the small bathroom to collect supplies—the tile is mint green, that much I can see from where I'm at. Then she goes back into the main room and returns with a chair from her small dining set from the kitchen.

She plunks the chair next to the edge of the bed, along with a first aid kit and a bowl of warm, soapy water and a washcloth. She sits down and takes my left hand and slowly washes away the debris. I try not to flinch, but it really hurts.

"I'm sorry I got mad at you earlier," I tell her.

"Don't be. I was being an asshole." She says sorry in her own way.

"Travis told me what really happened that night with Uncle Chuck."

She gives me an intense look before drying my hand. I watch as she puts some medicated ointment on my wounds and wraps everything with gauze.

"He was a son of a bitch." She shakes her head.

"Did Travis shoot him?" I have to ask.

"No..." she pauses and takes my other hand and starts cleaning it. For a moment I think she isn't going to say anything else. And I won't ask again. I'll leave it be. But then she opens her mouth. "The gun went off while they were wrestling around. I put it in Chuck's hand before Travis had time to blink."

"The police ruled it a suicide," I whisper and look at Justine. She's brave and fierce and strong. She's independent and smart too. She puts her head down on the edge of the bed and I take my bandaged hand and gently pet her hair. "Thank you." That's all I can manage to say.

The front door of her bungalow opens and I hear Mom call out for me. "RIAN!"

"She's back here, Tori," Justine lifts her head and calls out.

"Oh my God, Rian! What happened to you? Big Jackie said something about a panther and an alligator and—honey, just look at you. Should you go to the hospital? Look at that gash on your leg." Mom's eyes are scanning me for other injuries, just like Justine had done moments ago. Her hands are trembling and she looks like she hasn't had any sleep in days. Like when she used to prepare for a big case.

"No, I'll be alright Mom. I don't want to go to the hospital."

Darcy comes rushing into the room like a bat out of hell. Her ponytail waves furiously, she must have been running. "What happened? Where is she? Should I call an ambulance?"

"I'm okay, Darcy, relax. I'm more worried about the panther," I say and try not to cry again when I think about what just happened out in the woods.

"PANTHER?" Darcy screams. "Oh my god. Rian, look at you, did you get attacked by a panther?" Apparently I really look like shit.

"No, a panther saved me from a ten-foot alligator. Someone needs to go out there and check on the panther."

"What?!" Mom and Darcy both shriek.

"Where's Sam? I need Sam. He will understand," I croak. Mom is shaking her head and has no idea what the hell I'm talking about. "Mom, go get Sam. He's with Travis. And you need to stay with Travis– he got really drunk tonight, he was upset because of his parents. That's why I ran off. I couldn't deal with what he told me. I was so angry for the abuse those boys endured and for everyone here. I ran into the woods, it was stupid, I know. But please, seriously, Sam has to go check on the panther. They are ultra rare– it can't die because of ME!"

Okay, yeah, maybe I've never been one to care about the well being of others before. But from the way Mom's looking at me, she knows I'm being sincere. I really can't stomach the idea of the panther dying on my behalf.

"I'll go, Tori. You stay with the girls," Darcy offers and walks around to give me a quick kiss on the forehead. "I'm glad you're safe, Rian." She leaves the room to find Sam and keep an eye on Travis.

"Rian, I'm so sorry." Mom is standing at the edge of Justine's bed. She picks up my foot and starts cleaning the dirt and sticker burrs and splinters from my bloody flesh.

"Don't feel sorry for me. Feel sorry for Sam and Travis and Justine. The years of abuse—" I choke out the words. Mom looks horrified. I wonder if she knows Justine walked in on Uncle Chuck killing her sister.

Oh my god. I look over at Justine who has silently retreated to the corner of the room. That's what Justine and Mrs. Day were fighting about. Not stupid pirate treasure! Justine wants to tell Mom.

"Tori, I need to tell you something," Justine's voice cracks. She looks at me. She's got tears in her eyes. I nod at her and lift up my bandaged hand, beckoning her to come out of the corner. I'll try to be strong for her.

"Are you okay, Justine?" Mom sets my foot down gently on the bed.

"No, not really. I mean, I don't know if this is the right time, but something's been eating me alive for weeks. I need to tell you what really happened that night your sister died."

Mom puts her hand on Justine's shoulder. And without any hesitation, Justine tells Mom everything. The years of terror– the lies Uncle Chuck told. The money he gambled away. The women. The drinking. All of it. Mom listens and goes back to cleaning and wrapping my knees and shins.

I close my eyes and let them have their moment together.

Mom doesn't cry. At least I don't hear any sniffles. And Justine stays strong even if her voice wobbles a few times. Based on her argument with Mrs. Day, some folks around here are worried Mom will be mad at them for not interfering and trying to stop Uncle Chuck.

Finally when the last bandage goes on, and a few minutes have passed, I open my eyes. Mom is hugging Justine. "Thank god he didn't kill you or Travis." That's when mom finally breaks down. "It's not your fault." She squeezes Justine even harder. "What happened in this house wasn't your fault." She says the words Justine has been so desperate to hear before her shoulders slump into Mom's welcoming arms.

"I'm sorry. I'm so, so, sorry," Justine whimpers, her body shaking as she cries.

Mom grabs her by the shoulders and pushes her back and looks at her. "You have nothing to be sorry for. You and Sam and Travis, and everyone here. You are survivors." She sweeps her into another embrace. "I tried for years to get my sister to divorce that asshole. I flew down here several times over the years and tried to get the sheriff involved to protect you and the boys. But, Kris said she could handle it and told me to back off. She must have known what he was fully capable of and that's why she waited so long before trying to leave him."

Wow.

Tears stream down my face.

I had no idea Mom had flown down here to help her sister. But, rather than get mad at her for not telling me, I just add it to the list of things I want to learn more about. The new Rian, she's going to be a survivor like Justine and Sam and Travis. She's going to be the kind of friend and cousin and daughter that all of these people want to have in their life.

I sink back into the pillow, watching Mom hug Justine, and I finally let out the breath I was holding.

25

GATOR TEETH AND FIRST KISSES

THE SUN IS BEGINNING to peek through the windows, and as tired as I am, I can't sleep. Mom's been sitting with me for the last hour and takes an extra blanket and tucks it around me.

"I'm going to run back to the house and find you some joggers and a t-shirt. Justine, don't let her look in a mirror." Mom teases. I roll my eyes. "I'll be back in a flash. Do you need anything else, Rian?"

"Can you bring my sketch pad and pencils?" If I don't draw what happened out there in the swamp right now, I'm not sure I'll remember every detail. I have to get this feeling off my chest and the best way is for me to draw it. "Thanks Mom, for everything." I reach my arms out for a hug. She does a double take. But, leans forward and gives me a hug.

"You're going to sketch with those hands?" Mom asks when she leans in. It feels good to hold on to her. I'm surrounded by people without a Mom in this place... I think I better remember that the next time I'm pissed at her. I am one of the lucky ones to still have parents.

"I'm sure I'll manage. See, I can still move my fingers." I wiggle them. She laughs. Not her fake laugh. Her real laugh, the one I haven't heard in a long time. It's music to my ears— one of the only places I don't seem to have cuts and scrapes, I realize. "I love you, Mom."

"I love you too," she says and gives me a funny sort of smile before leaving.

Finally, the house is quiet, and I'm alone with Justine. She sits on the edge of the bed and pats my leg. Her eyes are nearly as swollen as mine from crying. I want to tell her so much. Like how I'm amazed at her strength. And about how I heard Aunt Kris's ghost out in the swamp, because if anyone might understand, it's her. But, before I can say a single word, her front door slams open and shut. Jesus! There are too many people around here.

"Hello?" Justine shouts. Big footsteps come clamoring down the tiny hallway.

"RIAN! JUSTINE!" It's Sam and Big Jackie. They come rushing into the bedroom, out of breath and sweaty.

"Holy shit. It was crazy out there! So much blood," Sam exclaims.

I clutch at my heart. "Oh no, is the panther dead?" I shake my head and tears rush to the surface of my eyes, dripping across my cheeks, even before my cousin tells me what happened.

"No, Rian, it's okay. Shhhh...." He pats my leg. "The panther is safe. She's alive. But damn, she did a number on that gator."

I look up in an instant, reading his face, making sure he's telling me the truth. His eyes are round and he's bouncing from foot to foot. Sam's wired on adrenaline.

"We finished the job for her. Took its head clean off. Biggest gator I've seen in a looooong time." Big Jackie shouts triumphantly and strokes his beard. "We gonna take it out back and chop it up, gonna make gator stew and celebrate you bein alive and that gator being dead." He slaps Sam on the back with a big wack, then laughs.

"Jackie, for god's sake!" Justine frowns.

I laugh nervously. "I'm not sure I want to eat it, it tried to eat me."

"Oh, you just wait and taste it before you make up your mind," Big Jackie says with a wink. "Ain't nothing better than gator stew."

"He's right, it's good," Sam adds.

I just shake my head, I don't want to talk about food right now. I'm worried about the panther and her offspring. "Did you find the panther kitten?" I sit up in bed and ask Sam.

"Yeah, after the gator was dead, the panther climbed down from the tree and carried her kitten out of the woods. She'll probably find a new den far away from here," Sam explains. I can tell that he's disappointed she's going to leave the property. But, who can blame her? After all the trauma that's happened, I'd want to leave too if I was her.

"At least you know they are safe." Justine moves closer to me and stroked my cheek.

"She saved my life," I choke out the words. I'm so thankful that fucking alligator didn't kill the panther or her kitten. I'd have marched back out there myself and killed it if Sam and Big Jackie hadn't.

Sam takes a deep breath and finally looks me up and down. "Oh god, Rian, you got tore up." Then he inspects my leg where it's bandaged from knee to foot and resting on a pillow. "Did the gator bite you?" His lower lip trembles as he asks me.

"No, this was from falling on a stick, it sliced me pretty good. If the panther hadn't been there, I'd be gator food for sure." I'd laugh if it wasn't all so terrifying.

"Okay you too, I think it's time Rian gets some rest. Justine advocates for me. But Sam and Big Jackie seem hesitant to leave.

"Just wait until Travis wakes up tomorrow and hears that he missed the adventure. What a dumb-ass. I told him to stop drinking." Sam shakes his head. "I'm real glad you're okay Rian." He leans over the bed and scoops me into a hug. It's warm and comforting and he sniffles once, okay, maybe twice.

Of course I can't help it and tears freely stream down my face, hot and stinging my cheeks. "Thanks Sam. Me too."

Big Jackie and Sam leave shortly after that. Sam says he's going to make me a necklace from the gator teeth. Mom comes back to help me change. It feels good to be in clean clothes. She offers to take me back to my room, but Justine surprises the hell out of me and tells Mom she'd like me to stay for a while. Mom gives me the eye but agrees and heads back, I'm sure the Big House buzzes with all the drama anyway. I'd never be able to get any sleep with all the noise. Even on the second floor, with that many hens in the kitchen, it would be a clucking mess.

"I've ruined your bedding and sheets," I say to Justine once we are alone.

"It doesn't matter. Do you want to go sit on the couch and let me pick the leaves from your hair?" she asks.

I nod and she helps me up from the bed and out to the couch where we slump down together. She sits on one side and I lie across and put my head in her lap. She puts music on her phone then gently pulls out bits of torn palm and pieces of grass from my hair. And then she just pets me for a while. Feeling her softly stroke my hair, it's what I need. The calm after a storm. More like a hurricane, roaring and crashing around me, dragging me from the ocean into the swamps.

I know I should take it slow because I don't want to ruin my chances with her again. But, even in all the pain I'm in, I want to pull her down to me and hold her tight.

"Can I look at your sketchbook?" Justine asks after a while.

"Sure."

I sit up and take it off the coffee table where Mom left it for me. I carefully snuggle up next to Justine. Then I open it to the first page. It's odd, I've got so many sketchbooks, sometimes I forget what's in them. There's no real organization to any of them, I just draw my mood or something I've seen. Like Dad said. It's a hobby. But, the more I think about that, it kind of pisses me off. I mean, why couldn't art be my thing? I have every right to follow my dreams. What did Dad expect me to do when

I grew up? Become an actual New York Socialite? A trust funder with an empty, meaningless life?

We flip through the pages together, looking at city scapes and people I've drawn.

"Rian, do you know how good these are?" Justine asks. She traces the buildings gently with her finger.

"These pages are just rough drafts. I have a different sketchbook where I put more time and design into the pictures. Mom grabbed the one off my bed, the other books are in my desk drawer," I tell her.

"I want to see all of your work," she says and turns the pages. We get out of New York and into Florida. There's one of Sam with his million dollar smile. And one of Travis working on the car. She's about to see some sketches that might make her uncomfortable.

"Oh, you don't have to keep looking." I try to take the book from her.

But she pulls away and turns the page again. "Whoa, that looks just like us!" It's a sketch of her and Big Jackie out back that first day I met them beating on the rug and arguing.

"You don't want to keep looking," I say to stop her from turning to the next page.

"Why? What are you afraid of?" Her voice is husky.

"You..."

But she turns the page anyway. It's a sketch of her. With that face she makes like she's annoyed, but only teasing. She looks at it for a moment and smiles. Then she turns to the next page and it's her again. She turns another, the paper making a whooshing sound as it flips.

Page after page of her face, sketched by my memory, filled with longing and desire.

I've leaned in closer to her as she's analyzing each page, my head practically on her shoulder. My heart feels like it's choking me. When she reaches the last page, it's a sketch of the two of us standing in New York at Rockefeller Plaza during Christmas. She's wearing a peacoat with a fur collar and looking up to the snow filled sky. Pure joy on her face. And I'm holding her hand and staring at her, not the snow. Pure joy on my face.

Justine looks at me.

"Sorry, uh... you're just nice to draw," I say quietly and lift up to look her in the eyes. Those eyes! I am lost in them. "I hope it–" but before I can finish, she leans over and kisses me. It's everything I want it to be. Everything I need our first kiss to be. It's filled with hope and longing. It makes my toes curl, which is pretty hard considering how bandaged my feet are.

"You can draw me whenever you want," she says after she pulls her lips from mine. I don't say anything.

I just lean in and kiss her again.

26

SURPRISE VISIT

THE NEXT FEW WEEKS fly by because the house is a zoo. Mom's got a bunch of people here from New York helping optimize business operations at the fishing lure manufacturing plant. Darcy is in charge of managing the rebranding and launch party, not to mention she's been studying for her Florida bar exam. Mrs. Day, Mrs. Paula and everyone else who works here have been going crazy with taking care of guests and cooking and cleaning. It's really like living in a hotel now. And honestly, I don't mind it. The only part I hate is that Justine has spent all her time working.

Sure, we've had a few moments together—we watched a movie the other night with Sam. We helped Mrs. Day with flower arrangements. We rode with Mom into town to help her load up old paperwork from the office.

But we've had zero alone time.

Fortunately, we text a lot at night. Justine says it's good this way to get to know one another better. She's never had a real girlfriend before, I think it makes her nervous.

That or the fact we live at the same address. I guess it does put some extra pressure on a new relationship.

I try to occupy myself with other things. Like hanging out with Sam. Doing our usual things, like swamp fishing and mudding, which by the way is hard with the amount of bandages I'm still wearing. Travis isn't ignoring us, but he has been spending most of his time with Mom and her business associates. He's even been dressing up in suits and attending meetings. And according to Mom, he has a firm grasp on the family business. That twinkle in her eye tells me she's really proud of him, and even though it's not the same roaming the swamps without him, I'm proud he's stepping up to take an active role in the family fishing lure business. It is his birthright afterall.

"So, what should we do today?" I ask Sam after getting ready one morning and meandering down the hallway. Sam is sitting at his desk working on his computer. I lean against the door frame. "Mom sent a text– she'll be gone until dinner and Travis is with her again. So, you wanna go fishing? Or play ball in the barn before it gets too hot. I think my hands are healed enough that I can handle the ball."

"Nope. I've got something planned for you. Come on, it's in the library," he says and gets up from his desk.

"The library?" I ask hesitantly.

"What? Are you scared of books?" He teases and looks over his shoulder.

"No, I'm just not in the mood for reading a novel today," I tell him.

"Well, there is something you should see in the library. It doesn't involve reading, I promise. Please?" he begs me to follow him.

"Fine." I fold my arms over my chest. "But it better be good."

He smirks and smiles. "Oh, it is."

I follow him down the stairs and toward the library. I can hear Darcy talking to someone on the other side of the door. Hmmm. That's strange.

"Sam, perfect timing," Darcy says when Sam walks into the room ahead of me.

"What is all this about?" I ask, then I stop dead in my tracks when I see someone I really wasn't expecting. "Dad! What the hell are you doing here?" I demand as soon as I see my father. He looks different then I remember. It's been like four, wait, five months since I've seen him. I wonder when he got here?

"Rian, nice to see you." He shifts uncomfortably and comes toward me. Are we supposed to hug? I look from Darcy to Sam and back again at Dad. I'm surprised at the warm color in his face and the fullness of his dark hair. He looks more alive than I remember, and I guess I like it, but it's new and kind of startling. Like being away from me and Mom has given him a new lease on life.

"Uh, nice to see you too," I manage to reply right before he wraps his arms around me. I don't get my own arms up in time for the hug and it's awkward. I hate it. And I hate that he's here right now. But, seriously, what is he doing here? "Is everything okay, Dad? Where's Heather? Does Mom know you are here?" I step back and look over at Darcy. She nods and my heart relaxes for a split second.

"Yes, your Mom knows I'm here. And Heather is fine. I left her at our hotel in Miami." He shits from foot to foot. "We had to fly back to the states to sell her condo and finalize some paperwork; there is a lot of paperwork when you make an international move." He chuckles nervously. "Plus, I wanted to come see you in person."

"Wait? Like you're moving to Germany permanently?"

Is he serious? I thought he was going home to New York at the end of the summer. I thought he'd buy a new apartment with Heather, one with an extra bedroom for me. He is my back up plan! He's supposed to be my safety net, you know just in case things here don't work out. He's... he's... my Dad. How can he move to another country? A knot forms in my stomach and I rub it, as if that will help.

"Well, my office has decided to open a branch in Germany and they want me to head it up," he says sheepishly.

"I see." I whisper and slowly move my arms up and wrap over my chest, biting my lip to keep from crying.

"I– well, there's something else too." He looks around at Sam and Darcy, who are silently watching this entire scene unfold, from their spots in the overstuffed leather chairs. After what feels like forever, he looks back at me and reaches for my hands, but it's really weird. I don't reach out for him. I mean, come on Dad! Like I'm not some little girl anymore.

"What is it Dad? Spit it out. It can't be that bad." I use my best New York attitude. "I mean, you're moving to

Germany with Heather. What else could there be? Did you and Heather get married? Is that even legal? Is your divorce with Mom finalized?"

"Good guess." He nods. "Actually, we are getting married next spring. But, what I really wanted to tell you, in person, is that we are having a baby. Two. Two babies. Twins." More nervous laughter.

My jaw hits the floor. And I don't say a damn thing.

So, Dad keeps going after he rubs his hand across his hair. "Heather is pregnant with twins. That's why I accepted the permanent position in Germany. Heather's grandparents live in Berlin and she wants the twins to have dual citizenship– so we bought a house." He pauses to shrug. "We are going to raise them in Europe." He finally stops talking when he sees my face. I'm trying my hardest not to let it twist up. But, what was that thing Dad always used to say to his asshole friends at dinner parties? Oh yeah, people with more than one child are a burden on society. Funny right?

"Wow, twins. That's so exciting," Darcy says, trying to lighten the mood. "Isn't that exciting, Rian? You'll be a big sister!"

"Twins run on our side too. Gramps had twin brothers, there's an album with some old pictures somewhere," Sam says and gets up and opens one of the cupboards in the back of the library.

I smile. I love Darcy and Sam right now. They are filling my silence with words. Letting me process this moment, giving me time to figure out how to react. I guess I could behave like a NYP. Maybe that's why Dad came here in person, to see me blow up, just to hear my voice and see my lips move when I tell him how irresponsible and gross it is. He's like in his fifties! I mean, sure Heather is thirty something. But still, will he even see these kids grow up? I mean, he sure wasn't interested in me when I was growing up.

I open my mouth. Then I close it. I squeeze my eyes shut. I need to think, without Dad staring at me. I have two options. I can A) blow up and be exactly the girl my Dad raised me to be. Or B) I can be supportive of his new life, just like I always dreamed he would be of me, supportive and loving. Maybe this is his second chance. Like, look at Mom. Florida is her second chance. And me. This place is my second chance too, so what better way to prove it to him. I open my eyes and look at him with a genuine smile.

"I'm really happy for you, Dad," I say softly and wrap my arms around him for a real hug. This time I'm ready and so is he. He embraces me, and I let myself take in his familiar smell. Something I'd forgotten and I kind of needed. He smells like soap and nutmeg. He chuckles and I can tell he's not sure if I'm being serious. So I hug him harder and whisper, "You're going to be a really good Dad, *this time*. Think of me as your practice run." His shoulders relax and his grip around me tightens.

"Oh, Rian, thank you," he practically sobs. Yeah, yeah, okay. I can only handle so much mushiness from my Dad. I loosen my grip and pull myself out of our super sweet, but also super long, hug.

"You wanna tour of the place? I mean, as long as you're here. Mom's in town with her business advisors at the fishing lure plant. Or, we could go have brunch, I know a place," I say with a smile. Maybe it's just me, but Dad suddenly looks a hell of a lot more like himself. Like a huge weight has been lifted and he's comfortable in his own skin again.

"I'd like that Rian... Let's go have brunch. Then I'll have to get back to the hotel. Heather and I are flying up to New York tonight. We only landed in Miami yesterday so I could see you."

Looking at him, and studying him, I know he's not the same man who was my father growing up. The wrinkles that used to weigh down his forehead are gone and there is a light in his eyes. Spending time with this version of him doesn't seem all that bad. He doesn't seem hard and angry and bitter around the edges like he used to when we lived together in New York. And he hasn't even looked at his phone once or said anything snarky or demeaning.

"Okay, let me grab my phone, then we can go. I'll meet you by the car." I look over at my cousin. "Sam, will you come with me upstairs? I need to talk to you before I go." Why is he still digging in a cupboard for a long-lost family photo album?

He looks over his shoulder, then stands, "Sure thing, cous" he says, relieved to be leaving the library.

I shut the door after we walk out, leaving Darcy with my Dad.

"I think you're taking this pretty well," Sam says as we walk up the stairs.

"Yeah, I figured I could throw a temper tantrum like a baby. But, it's his life, I should be supportive. I mean, I'm nearly seventeen." I pause mid-step, my hand reaching for the banister, and think. "Oh wait, actually, today is my birthday."

I start to laugh. I'd completely forgotten, and apparently, so has everyone else around here. I said something to Justine about it last week, and that was the last time I'd even thought about my birthday. The old Rian, the New York Princess Rian, she would have been planning a party for weeks. Months even!

But the new me, honestly it doesn't even matter. I'm not mad that no one remembered, birthdays are over-rated anyway, right? Okay, so maybe I'm a little hurt that Mom didn't say happy birthday to me before she left this morning. Or that there wasn't breakfast in bed. Or a new dress or something.

"Did you say today is your birthday? Oh man, cous, I'm so sorry I forgot. Happy Birthday," Sam says quickly. But, there's a twinkle in his eye and something in that southern drawl of his, something sneaky... I narrow my gaze on him and step closer. He backs up, nearly knocking the picture of Gramm Tweety off the wall. He looks up toward the ceiling and refuses to make further eye contact with me.

"What did you say?" I demand.

"What? Happy Birthday?" His voice goes up an octave. Yep. He's definitely up to something.

"Sam," I say. And poor Sam, he looks right and left, but there's no one on this staircase who can save him. He laughs and rubs his hand through his hair. I notice a bead of sweat dripping down his brow. He's totally caught. Hmmmm... I wonder what he's planning? A surprise for me– of that I'm certain. But, I wonder what kind of surprise?

"Don't you gotta get your phone? Your Dad's waiting for that brunch you promised him. Better get going," Sam says awkwardly and dodges away from me, running the rest of the way up the stairs to his room and slams the door shut.

I shake my head and smile. Sam is too easy to break. I hope whatever he's planning involves Justine and some time away from the house. It's been so crazy here, and now, this thing with my Dad. I think I might still be in shock. I run up the rest of the stairs and get my phone. No messages from my friends. But, that's okay, it's still pretty early. One thing about Ava, Maggie and Gina, those girls love to sleep in during summer vacation.

I practically skip out the front doors and hop into Dad's rental car, thinking of the possibilities for whatever Sam was hiding.

"I'm pleasantly surprised to see how well you're doing here," Dad says to me as he cruises slowly down Old Palmetto Drive. He goes slow, not like Justine and definitely not like Travis.

"Yeah, me too actually. The first week was kind of rough, but I really like it here." The words are authentic as they come out. Because I really mean it. I like it here.

"I always had my doubts about this place. I mean, what your Mom went through with Samantha. And god, that SOB Chuck. I mean, I don't usually curse the dead. But that guy was the biggest piece of shit." Dad shakes his head.

I wave happily at Robert as we pass the gate. He nods his head at me and Dad.

"So, you knew about Samantha?" I turn and ask dad.

"Of course I did. I was married to your mom for twenty years, Rian. There's not much I didn't know," he gives me a sideways kind of look.

"Oh. It might have been nice for you and Mom to tell me about this part of her life." I sink back into my seat.

"Which way are we going?" he asks when we get to the main turn.

"Turn left, it's like thirty miles to a shitty looking strip mall with neon signs. There's an old diner and they make the best bacon, eggs and pancakes on the planet."

"Jesus, Rian. Thirty miles? They better be phenomenal pancakes," he teases.

But, the miles go fast and he talks the entire time. He tells me about Germany and how I can come visit anytime I want. He describes the house they just bought with a big yard so he can build the twins a swingset when they get older. He says he's sorry he fucked things up when I was a kid.

I nod and say things like, "That's nice Dad" and "Wow, how exciting." I'm trying my hardest not to fall back into my snotty privileged ways, meaning I'm not saying what I really feel, which is that Dad's being kind of selfish— holding out all this Good Dad stuff for the twins.

As I keep listening, I realize in a roundabout way, he's trying to ask for my forgiveness. Fortunately, before I have to answer his request, we reach the strip mall and the greasy diner where me and Justine ate breakfast. I point and he pulls in off the highway and parks in the same spot me and Justine parked in.

I reach for the handle to open the door.

"Rian, wait. I have something for you," Dad says and leans into the back seat of his rental car. I didn't even notice he had anything back there. He pulls a nicely wrapped present forward and holds it carefully.

"You remembered?"

"How could I forget your birthday? My princess is seventeen. You've really grown up and blossomed, Rian. A year ago, we hardly spoke. And if we did, you spent the entire time complaining about something trivial. Now, you are thoughtful and a great listener. I'm proud of you." He smiles and hands me the gift. I look at him and stare and blink a few times. Then I shake my head.

"God, you sound just like Mom. She loves comparing me to a flower in bloom."

Dad lets out a laugh. It's warm and sincere.

"You're both giving me a complex. I mean, was I really that bad back in New York? I mean, you both kind of spoiled me and gave me anything I wanted. So, if I had a bad attitude, I'm not the one to blame." I point out the obvious.

"Yeah, I guess we did," Dad scratches his head. "Never mind that. Go on, open it." He grins as he looks from me to the present and back again to my face. I can tell he's excited for me to see the present he brought.

I'm nervous. No matter what is inside this box, I have to tell him I love it. Which is something I'm not very good at. Normally I am the first one to tell my parents when they give me a shitty gift. But, this is the new me.

I'm alive. Not food in the bottom of a gator belly. And I'm happy to be alive. Right?

So I slowly open the expertly wrapped gift box and take the lid off and pull back the tissue paper. It's a picture of my future siblings bedroom with two designer cribs and some expensive one-of-a-kind mural by some fancy German artist on the wall behind them.

"Uh thanks," I mumble. Is he trying to rub it in my face just a little harder that he's left us and is starting a new life? I take a few quick breaths to calm myself down.

"Rian, I can tell you are confused. Just look at it. Really look at the painting," he urges.

"I don't see what the point is." But for his sake, I look at the wall behind the cribs, searching the mural for an artist mark. It's painted like a sketch, using charcoal in varying shades of gray, a good use of the light and dark. "Wait? Is that–" I pause.

It's one of my sketches painted in the twins' room.

From that day– the one in Central Park when me and Dad were there during a medieval festival. Seriously not our scene, but we walked around anyway, just for something to do. Dad took a call with someone from his work and left me sitting on a bench on the far side of the festival. There was a little girl, dressed in a princess costume chasing beams of light scattered between the maple trees. Thank god I had my sketch book, because it was such a beautiful moment, I felt like I was a thousand miles away in a fairytale. And even though I was upset Dad had left me there alone, I sketched the girl and the joy on her face and it made me happy.

Then after his phone call Dad came rushing back, "Rian, Rian!" he shouted for me. I remember the way I felt, looking up from my sketch pad, seeing him run toward me with two wands of fluffy pink cotton candy.

Later that night I finished my sketch. It wasn't a nameless girl, it was me, and Dad was a knight in shining armor, swooping in to slay the dragon. I *never* sketch fantasy, you know, fairies and wizards. I am absolutely not into any of that.

But, that day, it was magical.

I can't really explain it.

Looking at the framed photograph, and seeing my sketch painted in full scale, I almost can't believe it's something I created. The movement in the lines of the trees and the light catching the shapes and the emotion. I'm choked up by all of it. And Heather! What a bitch. I mean, in a totally good way. Like, I didn't think she even liked me. But, I guess she likes me enough to hire some painter to put my art up on the wall of her babies' room. My future brother or sister, or both.

"God, Dad!" I sob and look at him.

He's crying too.

I lean over the middle console of the car and hug him. This is the best birthday present he could have given me. I mean, I thought he didn't take me or my art seriously before this moment. But, now, he looks proud of me.

"I wasn't sure if you'd be mad that I took your sketch and let someone paint it on the wall," he says when we finally let go.

"No I'm not mad! I think it's really amazing." I smile and sniffle and try to wipe my face. I'm sure I look like shit now, but I don't care. It was worth it.

My stomach makes a grumble and we both laugh.

"Should we eat?" He asks.

"YESSSS! I'm starved!"

27

PROUD OF WHO YOU ARE

DAD AND I HARDLY manage to eat we are so busy talking and catching up. He is impressed with my black coffee drinking skills. He says it's very European. Which leads into a segway about me going to visit after the twins are born. Which, uh, yes! I tell him all about Cullier Manor House and what really happened the night Aunt Kris died with Justine and Travis.

"Man, I knew Chuck was a dirtbag, but to kill his own wife and try to kill Justine and Travis too. Those kids are lucky to be alive," he says and shakes his head.

"Is that why you and mom never talked about Mom's side of the family?" I ask.

"You know, it just sort of happened. We didn't have some big plan to keep her past from you," he says and takes a sip of his coffee. "After your Mom finished law school, and we'd decided to stay in New York, she just let that side of herself fall away. I think she was worried that her clients and partners at the law firm would hold it against her."

I nod. I know New Yorkers.

We are kind of assholes.

"I'll admit, it was just easier that way, to pretend Tori was a New Yorker through and through– and after a while it just became who we were." He rests his elbows on the table, and steeples his fingers, rapping them against themselves. "I do seem to recall a few times I was probably harder on her than I should have been when her country side slipped out. And for that, Rian, I am sorry."

I have to digest what he just said. It's heavy. I swirl the butter on my pancakes with a knife, making circles, inside of circles, inside of circles, as I figure out what I want to say. Finally, I say the only thing I can say. "I forgive you, Dad. As long as you promise that from this day forward we are open and honest with each other. No more lies. No more secrets. I'm sick of them."

He reaches a hand across the table, clasping my hand, stopping me from swirling anymore butter. "Rian, I never want there to be secrets between us. I know I've not been the best kind of Dad. But, I tried, the only way I knew how." He chokes up. "You know, my parents died when I was young. I think that's part of the connection I had with your Mom. We were both orphans in a way. And meeting in New York, the city, well it embraced us. It became the center of our world."

"Yeah, Dad, I know." I look him in the eyes. "New York was the center of my world too, until the day Mom drove me down Old Palmetto Drive," I say it without being angry or bitter. I say it with hope and determination.

The front door to the diner opens and I turn to look. It's someone I recognize. Rushing in and pulling an apron over her neck.

"SORRY LIZ!" She shouts and grabs a coffee pot and starts at one end of the booths and starts working her way down. My cheeks flush for a moment. Because the one thing Dad and I haven't talked about today is about to present itself, if I know how these southerners are.

"Hey, you're Justine's *girlfriend*," Tara says. Yep, so this conversation is happening.

"Yeah," I say to her.

"You better treat her right. That girl is a survivor. She don't need no more bullshit," Tara says and fills up our coffee cups and walks away.

"What was that about?" Dad asks softly.

I shrug.

"Rian, I thought we said no more secrets," Dad reminds me.

So, I tell him everything about Justine. I spill my freaking guts. I'm so nervous how Dad will react, because back home in New York he always laughed and said me liking girls was just a phase. That I would grow out of it. He said according to his colleagues at work, all teenage girls crush on each other, but eventually marry their male college sweethearts.

Eye roll.

But, I'm proud to feel this way about Justine and I can't see it changing anytime soon. I don't want it to change anytime soon. She's my snowflake. Completely original. A sparkle in the night sky.

Tara walks back and puts the check on our table and gives me the eye. I smile at her and she winks. Dad leaves a fifty on the table, he always was a good tipper, and we get up and walk back to the car. Finally, after what feels like an eternity, he says, "I'm happy to know you are finally deciding who you really are, Rian. I think if Justine makes you happy and she respects you, then, she's probably someone worth calling your girlfriend."

"Really, Dad?"

"Really, Rian." He beeps the unlock on the car and we hop in. "I know you think you are, *or were*, a New York Princess. And there were certain expectations that came along with that title. But, honey, that was never a crown me or your Mom placed on you. I think, we both worked so much and you had a Nanny and we just–" Dad pauses and takes a deep breath. "I just hope we didn't screw you up too much. At the end of the day, all me and your Mom have ever wanted is for you to be happy." Dad wipes the sweat from his brow. The A/C in his rental isn't keeping up with the swamp heat.

I look at him and purse my lips. The man next to me is not the same Dad I grew up with. I'm jealous my new siblings are going to get this man. This reasonable, understanding, compassionate man!

"Dammit, Dad. I'm jealous of the twins," I say laughing and trying not to cry. I think I surprise him. Because he bursts out laughing too.

"What exactly does that mean?"

"It means, who are you and what have you done with my self-absorbed, Wall Street Dad? If you are the Dad the twins get, they are the two luckiest babies in the world." And I mean it with all my heart. Dad smiles as we drive out of the diner parking lot and get on the highway towards home.

28

ME, HAPPY? OBVIOUSLY!

"ARE YOU SURE YOU can't stay longer?" I ask when Dad pulls up to the Big House.

I want him to meet Justine and get to know Sam and Travis and everyone. I want him to have a real glimpse of my new life at Cullier Manor House.

"I'm sorry, Rian. If I'd known how much we both needed this, I'd have arranged our trip to stay longer. But, I really should get back or we will miss our flight. Heather can only travel for a few more weeks before it's not safe for her or the twins," he explains.

"Well, I'm going to take you up on the offer, to come see you after the twins are born. I'm sure it will be chaotic at first, so maybe when they are a few months old," I suggest.

"I can't wait, sweetheart. Heather is adamant we get some pictures of you and your siblings when they are little."

"I'd like that, some new family photos. Oooh, I'll go shopping in Miami and pick up matching outfits for the twins before the flight! They will be the most fashion-able babies in Germany."

"I wouldn't expect anything less from you Rian," Dad says. "I was thinking you might like to bring Sam and Travis and Justine with you. We've got plenty of room at the house. I'll feel less guilty about keeping you enter-tained if you have your cousins and girlfriend with you. I bet your Mom would appreciate a break from all of you teenagers. I can only imagine the trouble you four get into," he says with a smile and shakes his head.

"Thanks, Dad. I Love you."

"I love you too, Rian. Happy Birthday."

I get out of the car and make sure to take my gift, the picture frame of the twins mural. Probably the best gift I've ever been given; and that includes the time Mom gave me and the NYP's tickets to see Sam Smith at Madison Square Garden.

I watch Dad drive away and wave until his car is out of sight. Wait until I tell Mom about this. She will never believe me when I tell her how mature and supportive I behaved. Hell, how mature and supportive Dad be-haved!

"Was that your pops?" It's Big Jackie coming from around the corner of the house. He's covered in sweat and dabs at his head with a rag.

"Yeah, at least *he* remembered it was my birthday," I say and turn my nose up. It makes Big Jackie laugh. That deep warm laugh, the one I love. The one that stays with you for a long time. I'm not mad at him, he knows I'm teasing.

"Love that sass, little Miss Rian," he says and laughs again.

"You know, you are the happiest person I have ever met. I'd hate it, if I didn't like you," I tell him before running up to the porch.

"Ain't got nothing to complain about! You know Miss Rian, happiness is contagious." Then he heads back out to do whatever job he was working on before I got home, but he pauses. "And who said we forgot it was your birthday?" He winks at me.

I knew it!

My heart swells and I let out a sigh. He's right. So I look around, I don't see anyone. "HAPPINESS IS CON-TAGIOUS!" I scream it as loud as I can.

"Ain't that the truth!" Big Jackie shouts back and follows it with one of his swamp noises. "SSSKKEEESKKOOOO!"

God, how embarrassing. I thought he was far enough away not to hear me.

"I'm home," I shout when I get inside. I hear people and things happening. But, no one comes to say hello or to tell me happy birthday. So, I run upstairs to my room and I put the picture from Dad on my desk. When I pull it out of the box, I see there is a note in the bottom of the box, I'm not sure how I missed it in the car.

Rian,

I'm sorry if I ever made you feel less than perfect just the way you are. Paint the world as you see it.

Love, Dad

Before I can choke up and cry, again, there is a knock at my door.

"Come in," I say. I'm expecting Sam.

"Where did you take your dad? You've been gone most of the day!" Justine says and walks into my room.

"I took him for a nice long brunch." I smile at her.

"Oh, I see how it is." She comes over and puts her arms around me.

"What? I was hungry! And we had a lot of catching up to do." I hug her back. She smells like home. I breathe her in. I want to pull her over to my bed and flop down and hold her close to me. But instead I say, "Did you miss me?"

"Maybe." She lets me go slowly and picks up the picture from my desk. "What's this?" She asks. Nothing slips by her.

"It's from my Dad. That's the twins' room." I go over to my closet and take off my shoes and start looking for something else to wear.

"Twins?" she asks.

"Yeah, I guess Dad and Heather are having twins. Surprise. It's cool though, he's actually happy for the first time in like forever. And like your brother says, happiness is contagious. So, I'm excited for them."

"Rian, that mural, behind the cribs, is that?" she asks.

"You noticed faster than I did. They hired an artist to paint one of my sketches in the babies' room." I smile and pull the first dress from my closet. It looks like the one I wore on my first day here; the green and blue Dolce&Gabbana sundress. But, it's not the same dress. This one is slightly different.

"I told you I had one that looked the same as the one you ruined. I brought it up here while you were gone and hung it in your closet. A little gift." Justine takes it gently from my hands, pulls it off the hanger, and smiles. "You'll look better in it than me." She steps in closer and holds the fabric up to my body.

"You don't have to give me this," I say quietly, my breathing quickens.

"Yeah, I know, but I want you to have it." She bites her lip. "Will you put it on?" Her eyes sparkle.

"Right here?" I squeak. We are inches from one another. My body comes alive with the thought of getting undressed for Justine. She leans in and gently kisses my lips.

"As much as I'd love to watch you change, I can't stay. I have a few things to finish up before–"

"Before what?"

"It's a surprise. You have some time. Take a bath, fix your hair. You know– all the Rian things you love to do."

"What are you up to?" I say and frown at her. But, she's already walking away. I just follow her with my eyes as she puts the picture from Dad back on the desk and goes to the door. I'm scared to look away, like I might miss a second of her. She is so perfect and I want more, I want to scream at her to turn around and come back.

Before I can stop myself I rush across my bedroom and grab her and kiss her.

"I told my Dad you are my girlfriend," I say after we come up for air. "I hope you aren't mad at me. I don't know what this is between us, but it feels like something real and–"

"Stop talking, Rian." She kisses me again. "Yes."

"Yes what?"

"Yes, I'll be your girlfriend."

29

SWEET SEVENTEEN

I TURN ON MUSIC in the bathroom and sing along while I take a long bubble bath. It feels good to get the remaining bandaids and medical tape off of my feet and soak until my skin is pruned. After an hour I slowly climb out, a little woozy from all the steam, but I manage to lotion everything and blow dry my hair. The dress from Justine looks so much better on my frame than the original one did. This hugs my body in all the right places and even though I know it came from a discount store, I don't hate the way the fabric feels on my skin. Plus, it still kind of smells like Justine. I can picture her sliding it over her own head and the material touching her body.

The thought gives me shivers.

I pull my hair into a high ponytail so I can wear dangly earrings. I top it all off with a sweep of glittery eyeshadow and about twenty coats of my favorite Dior mascara. Yeah, Ava, glitter shadow. I snap a quick selfie to send her, just to see what she says. But then I change my mind.

She hasn't told me happy birthday.

Come to think of it, none of my girls from back home have said anything to me today. God, they are such bitches! I mean, I thought Ava might send flowers. And Gina and Maggie would have at least sent a text message. But it has been completely silent on the friend front. Is this how it will be from now on? After being best friends for our entire lives, they've completely forgotten me on my birthday.

Before I can get worked up and seriously annoyed I hear the bell for sweet tea on the porch. Is it really 4 p.m.? Wow, the day has flown by!

"Rian, slow down," Darcy says as we nearly collide in the hallway.

"I'm late," I exclaim. "Come on." I grab her arm. I can't help but notice she's dressed up and wearing the sandals I bought for her with Justine.

"Jesus, Rian, take it easy. You're going to make us fall," she shrieks as we go flying down the stairs. The faces on the wall of my dead relatives are staring at me, the corners of their mouths turned up with smiles.

"Today is my birthday. I'm going to have a mint julep on the porch instead of stupid sweet tea."

"Oh really? You think Victoria will let you have a drink?"

I give her a look and she laughs. We both know Mom will cave after I ask once or twice. The house feels eerily empty as we rush past the library into the kitchen. Strange.

"Where is everyone?"

That's when I hear Mom laughing. She's out on the sun porch. Darcy opens the double doors for me and says, "Well, what are you waiting for? Go join your party. Happy Birthday, Rian!"

I rush through the doors and standing in the middle of the sun porch are three faces I wasn't expecting. Ava, Gina and Maggie. They didn't forget me! "SURPRISE!" They shout.

Before I can react, someone pops a bottle of champagne and music starts playing. Sam and Travis lead the crowd in a very country rendition of "Happy Birthday" and I can't help myself and burst into tears.

"RIAN!" Ava prances over to me.

"NYP's in the house!" Gina shouts.

"Your cousins are so hot," Maggie says, without even trying to hide her voice.

I wipe my tears and smile and laugh. "Sorry, I'm a mess. I didn't expect to see you. I kind of thought you forgot about my birthday," I admit to my friends.

"Your mom planned it all. She called our parents and flew us here on a private jet. Super posh," Ava gushes and gives me a big hug.

"I love your dress! Who is it, Escada?" Gina asks.

"It's mine," Justine says and walks up and puts her arm around my waist. "I'm Justine, Rian's girlfriend." My friends all take a step back.

"You're even hotter in person," Ava says first. Maggie elbows her. Gina shoots her an evil eye. "Well what? Those shitty pictures Rian sent didn't do her justice. Same for those two. I call dibs on the one with the cowboy hat. He'll fit nicely in my carry-on." Ava points at Travis and Sam.

Justine and I look at one another and start laughing. "See I told you she'd want to take Travis home with her."

Mom makes her way over after I've had my reunion with my friends. "Well, honey, are you surprised?" she asks. She looks a lot better than she did a few weeks ago. Like she's finally been getting some sleep. Darcy approaches with two wine glasses and hands one to Mom.

"It was so hard to keep this a secret," Darcy exclaims.

"I knew something was up this morning!" I slap at her shoulder. "Sam was acting all nervous and you wouldn't look me in the eye. But I did not expect a party like this!"

"I told you we could pull it off, Tori," Darcy clinks her glass with Moms.

"I cannot believe you flew the NYP's here to celebrate with me." I'm trying not to cry again. "Seriously, thank you Mom. Thanks Darc. This is amazing."

I take another moment to look around. On the edge of the outdoor patio, there's a bunch of tables set up. One of them boasts a four tiered birthday cake with white and pink frosting roses. Another holds a huge pile of presents. The rest are covered with food. There's ribs, chicken fingers, and salads. Servers dressed smartly in black and white suits walk around, some with puff pastry appetizers on silver platters and others hold trays of champagne. There's even a wooden dance floor, assembled on the side lawn, under a cascade of twinkle lights and border of helium balloons.

"Happy Birthday, cous." Travis finally saunters over and tips his cowboy hat at my friends. "Ladies," he says and winks. Oh Lordy. He's definitely looking for trouble tonight. Ava and Gina giggle and fawn over him. And where did Maggie go?

"Look," Justine points to the dance floor where Sam and Maggie are dancing. He's spinning her and I swear I can see little heart emojis floating off of them. "That happened fast." I look over my shoulder, Mom is still hovering close.

"Mom, I'm not sure you thought this through. Ava, Gina and Maggie with Travis and Sam. I hope you realize the NYP's might never go back to New York. Cullier Manor House is never going to be the same after this weekend!"

"Rian, this place needs it. It's meant to be filled with laughter and the joy of young people. There have been enough serious nights and trauma to last us all a lifetime." Mom takes a few steps closer to me and puts her hand on my cheek. "Go, dance, party with your friends. Have a magical birthday tonight." She smiles, that wicked happy smile. The one I used to hate. But tonight, I love that smile on her, because it's for me.

"Thanks again, Mom. I love you." I flash her my best smile, it might not be as powerful as hers, but it's from my heart.

"I love you too. Now go, looks like the dance floor is heating up." She doesn't have to tell me twice. I grab Justine's hand and drag her with me.

"Are you ready for this?" I ask her.

"Yeah, are you ready? I've got some pretty sweet moves," she teases and pops her hip to the left with the beat of the music.

"Oh, you have no idea. Me and the NYP's used to go dancing all the time." I wiggle as I pull her along and she laughs.

"I bet you did," she says.

"Play Bette Davis Eyes!" I shout at the DJ. "This one's for you." I give Justine a kiss and squeeze her hand.

Travis, Ava and Gina are on the floor dancing with Sam and Maggie. Every one of them is laughing and smiling. I literally had no idea either of my cousins had moves like that. Wait until I grill them about their dancing the next time we are out on the boat. I laugh, thinking about them practicing out in the barn. Or maybe Justine gave them lessons. A bead of sweat rolls down the back of my neck and honestly, I don't care how hot or swampy it is tonight. There is no place I'd rather be than here with all of the people I love, twirling and two-stepping. Who would have guessed the day Mom and I drove down Old Palmetto Drive that I'd find everything that was missing from my privileged New York life.

Acknowledgements

I wrote this book from the notes I'd made in a silver sparkly journal I kept in the side bag of my pink bicycle. Me and my kids would ride to the park, they'd swing and play, while I sat on the bench and wrote little bits and pieces about a spoiled girl from New York. A girl who found herself in the wilds of the Florida Everglades, with nothing to do, or so she thought until she took a ride mudding in the swamps. Remember, life is what we make of it, no matter where we are.

There are many people I'd like to thank for helping me bring Rian and her journey to life.

First, I have to thank my loving husband and children for supporting me during my long nights and weekends of writing, revising, and editing. You inspire me and you are my reason. I swear, if it's the last thing I do, I'll give you all that 'Celebration Life' we've been dreaming of.

To my Daddy... I love you more than all the stars, because they go on forever and ever.

To Abigail Wild for continuing to take a chance on me and believing in my words and characters. Your faith in my ability brings tears to my eyes. I can't wait to see what we do next.

To Brittany McMunn and Nicole DeVincentis for your editing genius! Thank you both so very much. Editors are truly the unsung heroes of any good book.

To Dana Hawkins for being my joyful friend and cozy writing partner. Hugs and love forever!

To Amy Nielsen, my cheerleader extraordinaire! I can't thank you enough for your friendship and support.

To Ginny Myers Sain & the Sunday Girls, thank you for the giggles, stories, and uplifting messages.

To Theresa Green, you've taught me more about writing than I'll ever be able to thank you for! I'm so grateful to have a home with you and the Writer's Workout crew.

To E.L. Johnson, my darling friend from across the pond. Thank you for our video chats and writing sprints.

For all my Wild Ink Publishing & Conquest Publishing siblings... y'all are insane, and I love you, never change.

To everyone else in my life– my Nebraska/Iowa/Washington families, my BRPSC family, my friends on X, you all know who you are, and I thank you and love you for your encouragement.

About S.E. Reed

S.E. has lived in all five-regions of the United States which gives her a unique American perspective. Many of her pieces have a strong Southern theme, but she also dabbles in the strange, bizarre, and fantastical.

Her debut novel, MY HEART IS HURTING, won the 2024 Silver Medal in the Florida State Book Awards as well as the 2024 Paterson Prize for Books for Young People. Her short fiction has been nominated for a Pushcart Prize and she's won honorable mention twice in the L. Ron Hubbard Writers of the Future contest.

S.E. resides in Florida with her family– nestled between the swamps of the Everglades and the salt of the Atlantic Ocean. This summer she'll be sitting in a lawn chair, working on her next novel and listening to EDM...(Ask her about her days as a DJ). Or she'll be in the pool begging her kids not to get her hair wet.

www.writingwithreed.com

www.ingramcontent.com/pod-product-compliance
Lightning Source LLC
Chambersburg PA
CBHW060713190726
48289CB00002B/659